MW01134669

RESCUING LEAH

 FriesenPress

Suite 300 - 990 Fort St
Victoria, *BC, V8V 3K2*
Canada

www.friesenpress.com

Copyright © 2021 by Joey Janson
First Edition — 2021

All rights reserved.

No part of this publication may be reproduced in any form, or by any
means, electronic or mechanical, including photocopying, recording, or any
information browsing, storage, or retrieval system, without permission in
writing from FriesenPress.

ISBN
978-1-5255-9857-9 (Hardcover)
978-1-5255-9856-2 (Paperback)
978-1-5255-9858-6 (eBook)

1. *FICTION, ACTION & ADVENTURE*

Distributed to the trade by The Ingram Book Company

RESCUING LEAH

JOEY JANSON

CHAPTER 1

t was Leah's last day with me before leaving for four years of college. We were both sad, so we went to a driving range to hit some balls. It was our way of not talking about her departure because we both felt awkward. We'd become so close over the five years we'd been together. But we knew she had to get her degree, so she could move ahead in life. I knew I'd see her a lot less now. She'd be living on campus at the University of Southern California which is a 45 minute drive from where I live.

We took our places among the other people hitting golf balls in their shorts, shirts, caps, and shades and did what we normally did. I practiced my swings, trying to drive the ball farther and more accurately. Leah swung . . . and missed.

I put a ball on the tee, lined up my driver, took a swing, and the ball flew ahead and landed at the 250-yard mark.

Leah took a swing and missed. She took another swing and missed. As much as she said she liked golf, she wouldn't be playing for the PGA anytime soon.

"This is so hard," she complained, as she always did.

"You'll get the hang of it. Watch what I do," I replied. I sat another ball on the tee, lined up my club, and a few seconds later, my ball went soaring into the clear sky, sailing out of sight.

"Is there a trick I don't know?" Leah asked after hitting the top of her next ball.

"No. It just takes practice. Remember?" I set another ball on my tee and showed her how to swing. "The idea is to keep your legs apart but even with each other. Keep your head down, facing the ball, keep your lead arm straight, and take a nice, steady swing. See?" I sent the ball off into the distance.

Leah hit her ball sideways, and it went into the pond beside us. She tried again, hitting the ground.

"OK," I said. "Your feet weren't even, and your lead arm wasn't straight." I got behind her to demonstrate. Putting my chest on her back, my head over her right shoulder, and my arms around her, I held her hands as she held the club. "All you have to do is—"

"Oh! Hello there," she said as she turned her head at me and giggled.

At that moment I didn't want to be on a driving range. I wanted to be alone with her anywhere but there.

"Don't get me started in front of all these people," I whispered. She laughed.

"OK," I said. "Relax your muscles. Keep your legs apart and even with each other. Keep your head down, looking at the ball. Don't take your eyes off it. Pull your club back up to your shoulder, keeping your arms as straight as possible until they're up to your shoulder, and then swing!" I moved Leah's arms around to show her the feel of using the club correctly. "Now try it like that."

I released Leah's arms and walked away. She took a couple of practice swings before hitting, and then she took a good swing at the ball and hit it perfectly! It landed at the one-hundred-yard sign.

"There you go!" I yelled.

"Yes!" Leah cheered.

"Do it again, and see how far you go this time."

Leah set another ball on her tee, took another swing, and hit the ball perfectly again. It flew straight ahead, but instead of landing next to the one-hundred-yard sign, it hit the sign with a loud thump.

"Great job, Leah! Other than hitting the sign, great job! Just remember, when you're hitting the ball, it's the geometry you put into it."

"Can you show me how to hit the ball again?" she asked. "I sorta forgot . . ."

"Um . . . sure." I put my arms around her back and put my hands on her arms. "Now, while you're swinging your driver, keep your legs apart and even, head facing the ball . . ." She leaned back and rested her head on my shoulder.

"I love you, Josh."

"I love you too, Leah."

"I'm really gonna miss you when I leave."

"I'm gonna miss you too."

She put her club down and turned to face me.

"Are you sure you're gonna be OK while I'm gone?"

"Yeah I'll be fine," I said. "I'll miss having you around, but I'll be fine. It's just for a few years, honey, and then school will be all over."

"I know."

"Nothing's gonna change between us, OK? We're still gonna be together. Besides, you'll be home for Thanksgiving, Christmas, and other holidays. You'll be here more often than you think."

"I just feel like I should wait a little longer to go back to college because being away from you . . ."

"Leah, Leah, listen to me," I said as I put both my hands on her arms. "I want you to go to college and get a degree, so you can have a good career and a good future. I know us being apart is gonna be hard on us, but it's for the best. Besides, we'll stay in touch. We can FaceTime, call, text. I'll even handwrite letters to you, like Forrest Gump writing to Jenny." We laughed.

"Josh, I don't think people write letters anymore."

I gave her a hug. "Hey, I'll even send you a Snapchat picture with a funny filter just to make you laugh when you need it. And maybe a funny TikTok video."

Leah grinned, shook her head, put one of her hands on my cheek, and kissed me.

"I'm gonna miss you so much."

"I'll miss you too. You know if you need anything, I'm just a phone call away."

Leah nodded.

"Let's hit some more balls," I said, trying to cheer us up. "See if you have the hang of it now."

This time her ball went to the 150-yard sign.

"Wow, nice shot! See? it just takes practice!"

CHAPTER 2

was in Leah's bedroom at her parents' house, helping her pack her clothes and electronics. Her dorm room was going to be tiny, so she planned to leave most stuff at home. Her parents, Frank and Karen, have a huge home in a gated community called Beverly Park. It has a tennis court and pool, five bedrooms, five bathrooms, a full basement, and a four-car garage. Leah's dad is a federal judge. Karen owns a fashion business.

Eventually, we all sat down for dinner. Karen had made filet mignon, asparagus, scalloped potatoes, and salad. She asked Leah to bless the food, so we all joined hands and bowed our heads.

"Dear Heavenly Father, bless this food that you have given us. Thank you for all the blessings you put in our lives, Lord. Most of all, we thank you for your love and comfort when we need it and that you are a loving God who is always around when we need You. We thank You in Jesus's name. Amen."

"Amen," we echoed and started eating.

"Mmm . . . Karen. This is so good," I said, smiling at her.

"Yes, thanks, Mom," Leah agreed.

Frank muttered something too, but pretty soon he began texting on his phone. It always annoyed us.

"So, Josh," Karen said, "how's everything going at the dealership?"

"It's been busy. I guess when you do body repair for a living, the job is never done. But I enjoy it."

"Well, you have a good work ethic. Leah told me you've bought a project car?"

"Yeah. A red '69 Chevy Camaro Z28 convertible."

"Frank, did you hear that?" Frank didn't answer. He was engrossed in his messages. Karen sighed. I tried to lighten up the conversation.

"It's got a 302 small block under the hood and a 5-speed manual on the floor. I bought it from a farmer. He'd had it sitting in his barn for thirty years, and he's never driven it. So, it needs a lot of attention. I'm going to restore it completely— engine, body, everything on it."

"Sounds exciting," Karen said.

"I always love watching you wrench on cars," Leah said, rubbing my shoulder. "It's . . . entertaining."

I chuckled. But when I saw the stern look on Frank's face, I switched the topic. "Frank, I saw on the news that you put a drug lord away today. For life. That must feel good."

"The jury did a good job," he said. "It was a stressful case for them. The sentence was appropriate." Frank was always discreet about his cases around me. In fact, he was pretty terse around me in general.

He turned to Leah. "I hope you're enjoying your dinner, sweetheart. I still can't believe you're going away to college."

"I'll miss you and Mom," Leah said. "I'm gonna miss Mom's cooking."

"We won't be far away," Karen patted Leah's arm. "I'm sure Josh will be happy to come see you sometimes too."

"Absolutely," I said as I rubbed Leah's hand. "Anything at all, I'll be there before you know it." Leah smiled and kissed my lips.

"I love you," she said.

"Love you baby," I replied.

As we ended dinner, we were all dreading the hardest part of the day: saying goodbye. *Hold it together, Josh*, I told myself. *Hold it together*.

Eventually, Frank and Karen walked Leah outside to her brand-new Honda Accord Touring. I gave them space to hug and say their final goodbyes before their daughter headed off to a whole new world. I couldn't imagine what Frank and Karen were feeling.

"Josh, are you coming over here?" Leah called.

"Yeah, get over here and join us," Karen said.

Part of me didn't want to join the circle of sadness, but I didn't want to be sad alone either. I grinned and walked over.

"We'll leave you two alone," Karen said, putting her hand on Frank's and walking back inside with him.

Leah started tearing up and she put her arms around my neck. "I'm gonna miss you so much, Josh."

"I'm gonna miss you too," I said.

"It's gonna be so weird not seeing you every day."

"I know, but I'll come see you. And you'll be back home for the holidays."

Leah got in the driver's seat, turned on the ignition, and hopped back out.

"By the way. I have something for you." Leah reached into her pocket and pulled out a black leather bracelet with cross charms.

"Aw, Leah!"

"It's a prayer bracelet. I want you to wear it when you're alone, so the Lord will keep you safe."

"Babe, I love it! Where'd you get it?"

"I made it."

"You made this? Wow."

"Give me your hand."

Leah wrapped the bracelet around my wrist. I grinned at her. "Thank you. Now, it's getting late. You'd better get going, honey." I walked her to her car, opened the door, and closed it behind her.

Leah rolled down the window and rubbed my cheek.

"Leah," I said. "Anything, anything at all. I will always be there for you."

"I believe you," she said. She waved goodbye and slowly drove out onto the street, honking and waving through the sunroof. I watched her sadly as she disappeared.

As I started over to my Pontiac, my phone alerted me to her text message: "'I knew I was gonna start crying once you disappeared in the rear-view mirror."

I'm gonna miss you, Princess, I thought.

"Are you coming back in, Josh?" I heard Karen's voice and saw her standing in the doorway.

I smiled and shook my head. "I'm heading home. Thanks again for dinner. I have to get up early for work."

"Why don't you stay a while? I just want to make sure you're OK."

"OK." I walked inside. In the living room, Frank was switching TV channels to see coverage of the sentencing. Karen poured herself another glass of pinot noir. She handed Frank some cognac and grabbed a Corona for me.

"You OK?" she asked.

"Yeah I'm fine."

"I know you're sad, Josh. We're all sad to see her go. But it's not like you'll never see her again. Besides, in every relationship, it's good to be apart from time to time."

"I know."

Frank turned off the TV and joined us.

Karen smiled at him, "We were just saying how much we're going to miss Leah.

"I'm going to worry about her, being down there at that big campus all by herself. She doesn't know anyone there."

"I'm sure she'll be fine, Josh," Frank said. "There's security down there. You two worry too much."

"I'm the boyfriend," I said, with rising anger. I felt like Frank was always brushing me off. "It's my job to worry."

"We're her parents. It's our job to worry too when it's necessary. I'm telling you, she'll be fine."

Frank left the kitchen and went into his office.

Frank and I didn't get along too well. He didn't get along with anybody honestly. He had always thought of me as just a punk kid off the street with a street-style car and a crotch-rocket motorcycle.

"I'm so sorry about that, Josh," Karen said. "That was so uncalled for."

"I'm fine," I said softly and took a sip of my beer.

"Josh, I know it's been difficult for you, not knowing who your parents are. I know you have anger toward them, and I don't blame you."

"Karen, I'm sorry, but I have to ask. Am I a burden to your family?" The second I asked that question, Karen sat her glass down almost hard enough to break it. "Don't you ever, *ever* ask that again, Josh. Ever! Why would you ask that?"

"Frank doesn't like me, Karen. He never has."

"You need to listen to what I say and not what he says. He just likes being a prick."

"He verbally abuses me every day, and I get tired of it," I said. "Remember the day I met him? Instead of saying something like, 'Hi, nice to meet you,' he said, 'I don't like punks with crotch rockets.' Even after everything I've done for Leah, it's like there's no

9

satisfying him. He shows no respect for me. No gratitude. I had enough of that growing up. I remember back at the orphanages I lived at, no love was shown to me or the other kids. It was always, 'Follow the rules, don't ask questions, don't cause trouble, and you won't get kicked out.' I don't even wanna mention what the homeless shelter was like."

Karen nodded. "I know . . . I know you have a lot of anger toward your parents for abandoning you when you were a baby. What they did was awful. But you know what? Look at you now. You graduated from high school, went to college, and got your automotive repair certificate while living at a homeless shelter. You're holding down a job and making very good money, and on top of all of that, you have a big heart. I can see why my daughter asked you out." I grinned and nodded as Karen continued. "Now I want you to think about all the things I said and ask yourself if you think you're a burden to this family."

I shrugged. "Maybe not?"

"Exactly. I really appreciate everything you've done for Leah. You're a real blessing that God has given us." I grinned . Karen raised her glass. "Here's to you for being a blessing to this family."

CHAPTER 3

went home and found some leftover pizza in the fridge and ate it with a soda. I always like a little comfort food before I go to bed.

I thought about how Leah's parents were living the American dream: independent, successful, and sitting on piles of money. The only thing I was loaded with was financial debt and hopeless dreams of being successful and independent. I lived alone in a small, white brick house. It wasn't a fancy place but at least I owned it, and it was in a good neighborhood. It may not have qualified for MTV Cribs, unlike Frank and Karen's house, but I liked it.

I had one vehicle to drive to work: a black 2006 Pontiac GTO. I also had the '69 Camaro, but it wasn't drivable yet. And I had a Yamaha R1M motorcycle. I lived a pretty standard life compared to Frank and Karen.

Anyway, about earlier, when Karen and I were discussing my parents. When I was only two days old, my mom and dad gave me up and wanted nothing to do with me. So, I was put in an orphanage, but I was never adopted. I stayed there until I was eighteen, and then I was transferred to a homeless shelter. I stayed there until I was twenty. Along the way I went to school and got a job. I'd been living on my own ever since. Basically, my youth was filled with nothing but stress, sadness, and trauma. I never looked for my parents because I always had anger toward them. As far as I knew, they never looked for me either.

I was doing OK on my own, and I wasn't alone now. I had Leah and her family. So, to me, life was pretty good. *I shouldn't complain,* I thought.

I was sleepy. I went upstairs, changed into my PJs and T-shirt, and lay down in bed.

On the nightstand was a digital picture frame loaded with photos of Leah and me. I stared at the changing images, and it made me miss her even more. The next few years would be difficult . . .

CHAPTER 4

t was Saturday. Another day, another dollar at the dealership. I was taking apart the back of a 2015 Ford Explorer that had been rear-ended. Christian rock was blaring inside my Beats earbuds, helping to keep me in my "zone."

As I removed the bolts from the bumper, I wondered how Leah was doing. I could barely keep my mind on the bumper. She was all I could think about. I was praying she was safe and surrounded by good people.

A notification went off on my phone. I walked over to my tool station where it lay. Leah had sent me a selfie, with hearts surrounding her head. She wrote across the image that she missed me. I always loved it when she did that.

My coworker, Steve, a man in his fifties, walked over to me carrying a cup of coffee and two glazed donuts. I took off my earbuds.

"So?" he asked.

"So what?" I said.

"You haven't said a word all morning, bro."

"I'm sorry. I don't feel like saying anything today." I put my phone back on the tool station.

"Ohhhh. OK . . . I gotcha." Steve held a donut up to my face.

13

"Will this make you say something?" I grinned, took the donut, and bit into it. He smiled. "So did Leah leave yesterday?"

"Yeah, she did. I'm just worried about her, that's all."

"You don't have to worry. She'll be fine. Does she know anybody there?"

"No. She hasn't even met her roommate yet."

"You need to relax and think positively. That's what's best for her and you."

"You have a daughter. You know how that feels."

"I do. And I do know how it feels. You know, my daughter started the same way at college. The first few weeks were tough but she started making friends and blending in with other people. Before you know it, they start loving everything about college. Leah will find the right group.

I nodded. "I suppose."

"Wanna give me a hand?"

"Yeah." We walked over to a tailgate he'd painted, lifted it off the stands, and carried it to the Ford F-150 he was working on. Then we hooked it back on and closed it.

"Thanks."

"No problem."

"I can honestly tell you this," Steve said. "Leah will have so much fun at college. I remember my days in college. I had a lot of fun and made tons of new friends. Mostly drunken shenanigans and pranks on professors we didn't like. Have you ever pulled a prank on a professor you didn't like?"

"Oh man. I did for graduation," I said. "I had a professor who taught English. Nobody I knew could stand the dude. One time he actually had the nerve to fail me on a homework assignment he'd given me just because I'd written with a red pen. At graduation a bunch of my friends and I got together and decided to put his car on four jack stands, so he couldn't go anywhere."

Steve laughed.

"He had to call AAA to get his car on the ground." I laughed. "Yeah, I did enjoy college, and I guess you're right. Leah will start loving it before long."

"Chin up, bro,'" Steve said. "The good Lord above may work in mysterious ways, but they are always for the greater good. And He is keeping Leah in good hands."

"You're right."

"Remember, God is good."

"All the time," I said.

"And all the time?"

"God is good."

He laughed. "Amen, brother."

CHAPTER 5

After work, I went to the outlet mall to blow off steam and buy some clothes. Leah and I liked to do that together almost every weekend. If we saw something we liked, we would get each other to try it on. If we liked the way it looked, we wouldn't be able to keep our hands off each other.

I missed her this time. At our favorite store, I saw our friend, Lisa, behind the counter.

"Hi, Josh!" she said.

"Hey, Lisa. Have my shirts and jeans come in?"

"I have them right here for you. So, how's Leah doing?"

"So far, so good," I said. "We've been texting back and forth non-stop all day."

"Aww, she misses you. You miss her?"

"Kidding me? I practically held onto the back of her car, telling her not to leave."

Lisa chuckled.

"I'm doing fine though. We're just both new at having a long-distance relationship."

"Yeah, I understand. But she'll think you look hot when she sees you again and you're in those clothes. See you next time. Tell her hi from me!"

"I will," I said. "Bye!"

A cold beer was waiting in the fridge when I got home. I popped it open and headed to the garage for my nightly detail work on my GTO. With Newsboys blaring on the radio. I set about shining the tires, cleaning the glass, buffing and waxing the paint, and finishing with a microfiber rag. I could easily work for hours without realizing it. In the back of my mind that night though was my expectation that Leah would get hold of me after her classes.

Finally, when I felt I'd perfected the paint, I stood back to admire myself in the shining black exterior and smiled.

Just then a FaceTime alert rang on my laptop on my tool bench. It was Leah! I touched the screen, and her beautiful, smiling face appeared.

"Hey handsome!"

"Hey there beautiful!"

"How are you doing over there by yourself?"

"I'm doing fine."

"I miss you babe," Leah said.

"I miss you too. Hey, guess what?"

"What?"

"I picked up my jeans and shirts today."

"You went to Buckle without me?"

"Yeah, I'm sorry, honey. It wasn't the same without you. Do you remember the ones I ordered?"

"Oh, yeah! I wish I was there, so I could see how good your butt looks in those jeans." She laughed.

I grinned. "That makes two of us."

Leah waggled her eyebrows up and down and I laughed. "So how's everything at school?"

"Fine. So far so good. My roommate's pretty cool. We have a lot of the same classes together. The downside is that it's only been one day, and I'm already buried in homework. I won't have a life for a while."

"I'm sorry, sweetie. Do you like your professors?"

"Yeah, so far. Time will tell! How are you doing?"

"I'm fine.

"You know what I kept thinking about yesterday after I left?"

"What?"

"The day we met. Remember?"

"How can I forget? Five years ago, at Starbucks. You were with all of your girlfriends, and I was sitting in the corner of the shop with my laptop, studying for my final exam. Out of nowhere one of the baristas came up to me with another mocha saying it was from a girl. I looked at the cup, and you had written on it, 'Hi, from the girl in the brown leather jacket.'"

"Yeah." Leah smiled. "I was wondering what you were going to do then."

"You know, it wasn't easy for me to approach you after you gave me that drink."

"You seemed pretty chill."

"Oh, believe me, I may have seemed fine on the outside, but inside I was nervous. As I was walking up to you, I was wondering how I was going to introduce myself. You know what I kept thinking?"

"What?"

"That there was no way you were single. I thought you were way too beautiful to be single. I thought I was swinging for the fence. Then after I said hello, we sat down together and talked for hours until the cafe closed. We had so much in common. We talked on the phone until four in the morning. The day I met you was the best day of my life. I went to work in a good mood the next morning—even though I was dog tired."

She laughed. "Were you jumping and spinning around the shop?"

"Jumping, spinning, singing. I was Mr. Sunshine."

Leah laughed. "You were singing too?"

"Like an opera singer! I could have signed up for American Idol!"

Leah grinned. "You're such a goofball, Josh." She blew me a kiss. "Well, I'm gonna have to go, babe. I have to get up early."

"OK babe. Don't work too hard."

"You do the same."

"I miss you, Josh."

"I miss you too, Leah."

"I'll FaceTime with you again tomorrow after my classes. I'll introduce you to my roommate."

"Sounds good. Goodnight, beautiful."

"Goodnight, handsome."

I ended the call and closed my laptop. I always loved having late-night calls with Leah. I don't know how I got so lucky to have her in my life.

CHAPTER 6

The next morning before I left for work, I was so happy to be able to talk to Leah as she was leaving for class. I told her to check in with me every so often throughout her day, just so I could feel better. She seemed pretty excited, and I felt excited for her.

Later at the shop, I unboxed the new rear bumper for the Ford Explorer and got ready to spray on primer. Steve was teaching a new employee—an eighteen-year-old, fresh out of high school—how to spray primer on an old fender and do bodywork. We had to keep an eye on this guy because he was a recipe for disaster. He'd only been working at the dealership for a week, and he'd already backed into a customer's vehicle, broken some tools because he was using them the wrong way, and then sprayed clear coat all over the windshield of a customer's pickup because he thought it would protect it from cracking. Only the Lord knew what could happen next.

"Remember, light coats," Steve said to the kid as he walked over to me. "Need help getting that bumper out of the box?" he asked.

"I think I got it," I replied. "How's the new kid doing?"

Steve lowered his voice. "Only the good Lord knows what he's gonna screw up today." We both laughed. "I don't know how he got hired here."

"Has he shown any improvement?"

"He's like a rookie baseball player in the MLB. He swings and misses. Swings and misses. I'm trying to be patient; I really am, but it's getting harder and harder every day."

"Do you want me to train him instead?"

"Do you have a death wish or something?"

"No, but I do have patience, which you kinda lack." I grinned.

Steve chuckled. "You're young, that's why. Wait till you're my age."

The kid looked up. "Hey, Steve? How does this look?"

Steve walked back to him. "That's good. Now, let that dry for a while. In the meantime, let's disconnect the spray gun, so we can clean the primer out of the can."

The kid tried to disconnect Steve's spray gun from the air hose with his skinny arms. Then he accidentally grabbed the trigger, spraying primer all over Steve's face!

"Oh my God! I'm so sorry!" the kid yelled. Then he dropped the spray can on the ground. It broke, and the can exploded, splashing primer all over Steve's clothes.

I tried to keep from laughing, but the sound of everyone else in the shop laughing was egging me on.

Steve glared at me. He looked like he was about to kill the kid. The hilarious part was that the primer was white, and Steve was black—and bald.

I decided to add to the laughter. "Hey. look everyone! It's Casper the friendly ghost!"

"You can train him!" Steve said. "I'm done!"

My phone started ringing on top of my shop cart. I thought it might be Leah, but it was a number I didn't recognize. I answered anyway. "Hello?"

"Is this Josh Daniels?" a man asked sternly.

"Uh, yeah. Who is this?" I responded nervously.

"This is Detective Kurt Davis with the LAPD. I'm calling about your girlfriend, Leah Rodriguez. Have you seen her or talked to her today? She never showed up for any of her classes.

"Uh no that can't be. I just talked to her this morning when she was leaving for class," I said. My heart started to race. Steve was trying to say something to me. I could see him mouthing words, but I couldn't hear him. I was going numb.

"Well, I'm sorry to tell you, but she never showed up," the detective said. "We're questioning everyone close to her and the people she knows at school. Her parents told me to call you."

"You've gotta tell me what happened! Please! What's going on?"

"We're trying to get answers to where she could be, and we're talking to her parents right now."

"Um, OK. I'll be right over."

After I hung up, I noticed I had three missed calls from Leah. Something was going on. I felt like I was going to throw up.

"Everything OK, Josh?" Steve asked, as he wiped his face with a shop rag.

I almost couldn't answer him. "I really hope so."

Then I got a text message from Frank: "Josh, please get over to the house immediately! It's about Leah! Something is wrong!"

CHAPTER 7

I drove straight to Frank and Karen's house. Three Ford Explorer police Interceptors were sitting in the driveway, and two cops were standing at the door. I screeched into the driveway and ran over to them.

"Are you Josh Daniels?" an officer asked.

"Yes!"

A cop opened the door. Frank and Karen were sitting in the dining room with five officers. Two of them were wearing suits and ties. Frank got up and walked over to me. "Josh, this is Detective Kurt Davis. He wants to talk to you."

The detective, a tall man in his fifties, turned to me. "Josh, we spoke over the phone. This is FBI Agent James Carter." Another tall guy about the same age nodded at me.

"Where's my girlfriend?" I asked, my heart pounding.

"We don't know," Davis said. "Take a seat, and I'll explain what we know so far."

We all sat down in the living room as Davis continued. "We're looking at a few things that may or may not be tied to Leah's disappearance. There was a report of an altercation in the parking lot close to her dorm. They checked out her car, and her driver's side window was shattered. Also, a campus security guard was found dead in the hallway close to Leah's dorm room with multiple gunshot wounds in his chest."

My stomach turned and I put my head in my hands. I was scared out of my mind.

"LAPD is at the campus doing an investigation," Davis said

"Do you know anything else?" Frank asked.

"I'm afraid we don't have any more at this time," the detective said.

I stood up and started pacing.

"Josh, when Detective Davis called you earlier, you said you spoke to Leah this morning," Carter said. "Do you remember what time that was?"

I pulled out my phone and looked back at the time when Leah called me.

"7;15."

"How did she seem when she called? Did she seem depressed at all? Angry? Scared?"

"She seemed normal."

Karen began sobbing, and Frank put his arm around her.

"Look, we'll do everything we can here," Davis said, standing up. "If we hear anything new, I'll give you a call. Please call me if you hear anything." David and the other officers left the house.

"I'll call some of Leah's friends," Karen said as she went into the home office.

I sat down, feeling like I was about to pass out. My mind was filled with ideas of Leah being kidnapped, raped, or killed.

"We'll find her, Josh," Frank said. "Don't worry." He followed Karen into the office.

I speed-dialed Leah's number, but no one answered. I got her voicemail instead. "Hi, you've reached Leah Rodriguez. Leave your name and number, and I'll get back to you."

"Babe! Please call! I've been trying to get a hold of you. People can't find you. Call me as soon as you get this message. I love you. I . . . I hope everything's OK. Please call me."

CHAPTER 8

called Lisa at Buckle, the jeans store, and told her about the situation. She wanted to talk to me in person, so I dashed out the door and hightailed it over there.

"Lisa?" I started as I raced in the door. "The detective told me a security guard was shot dead in Leah's dorm hallway, a fight broke out outside her dorm, her car window got smashed . . ."

"Are you serious, Josh? This isn't a joke, right?"

"No! This isn't a joke! We're in trouble. Something bad has happened. The police are there investigating right now. If you hear anything at all, if she calls you, let me know. You have my number."

"Yeah, absolutely, Josh. Keep me posted."

"I will. Thanks." We hugged, and then I ran to my car.

CHAPTER 9

was up all night, panicking, praying, and asking myself over and over, Where could Leah be? Why wasn't she answering her phone or any of my texts? Was she hurt?

At home I sat and stared at my phone on the coffee table. I decided that if I didn't get an answer by morning, I would drive to the campus and have a look around. I would take matters into my own hands.

As I walked to the fridge to grab a soda, I heard the sound I'd been waiting for. I ran and saw Leah's name on the caller ID.

"Leah? Babe, where are you? Are you OK"

"This isn't Leah. I have Leah," a guy's deep voice said. Gripped with fear, I set my soda on the coffee table and switched my phone from my right ear to my left.

"Who the hell is this"

"You don't know me, but I know you," the man said in a Latino accent. "So tell me, Mr. Daniels, how much do you love your girl-friend? Are you willing to risk your life to save her?"

You son of a bitch, I thought. "Where's Leah?"

"She's OK. She's not hurt. Now, allow me to introduce myself, Josh. I'm Alonso Matias."

"Who are you, and what the hell do you want?"

"I want my father out of prison."

"What? Your father? Who's your father?"

"He's that man who your judge friend put away for life on Friday. I'm sure you know what I'm talking about."

My heart pounded so violently I thought I would have a heart attack.

"Pretty little girlfriend you have there."

"Josh!" I heard Leah scream from a distance.

"Leah!" I couldn't help yelling back, though she couldn't hear me.

"Now, Josh, I've already called Judge Rodriguez about his daughter. I just let him know I'm gonna kill his little girl."

"If you even scratch her—"

"I think you already get the picture. I can do whatever I want, wherever I want, with just the flick of my fingers. Starting now I'm giving you and Judge Rodriguez the option of getting my father released. If my father doesn't walk, you know what will happen. I will destroy your whole life. I will kill your pretty girl here. I will kill her parents, everyone you know, and then I'm gonna make sure you die, nice and slow."

Alonso hung up.

"Oh my God!" I said. "Oh, Jesus no!"

CHAPTER 10

raced over to Frank and Karen's house.

"Frank! Karen! Open the door!"

In seconds Karen stood facing me, in tears.

"Someone kidnapped Leah!" she yelled.

"I know!"

"What? You know?"

"He called me too!"

She burst into heaving sobs and put her arms around me. "They have my baby girl!"

I felt powerless. I was scared too.

"Who are these people?" Karen asked as she unwrapped herself from me.

"They're involved with that drug lord Frank put away on Friday. Where's Frank?"

"He's on the phone with Detective Davis."

Frank came darting down the staircase, yelling at Detective Davis on the phone. "Listen to me: my daughter's been kidnapped! This person isn't someone off the street! This is the son of Javier Matias! I need your help! He's threatening to kill her and my whole family!"

Frank looked stunned. He went quiet and held the phone at arm's length, staring at it. He looked at us incredulously. "He hung up on me!"

"He hung up?" Karen yelled.

"Are you kidding me?" I said. "Give me the phone, and I'll call the prick for what he is!"

"That's not gonna do any good, Josh!" Frank said.

"Why?"

"Because he knows who we're dealing with! That's why!" Frank's face was bright red. He put his hands on the back of a chair and leaned against it. "Oh my God! I never should have taken this case!"

Goosebumps went up my spine.

"Frank," I said, trying to keep myself from yelling at him. "What do you mean?"

"Damn it!" he yelled. "When they brought Javier Matias in, his attorney tried to bribe me. No one has ever wanted to sentence this guy, but I took the case knowing the possible consequences. I wanted to show what I could do with my authority, so I put him away for life! I put my baby at risk . . . my whole family."

"What?" Karen screamed. "Oh, my God. Oh, my God . . ." she doubled over, clutching herself, sobbing.

I had no words. I stood staring at Frank in fear and rage. My anxiety was through the roof. Karen straightened up and looked at Frank, stunned, like she didn't know who he was anymore.

Together, in silence, we looked at one another, wondering what we were going to do.

CHAPTER 11

t was nearly midnight when I left Karen and Frank. I drove home, distraught, and sat in my kitchen. I wasn't just going to pray to God that Leah would be OK because Leah could die if I did only that. I had to find her. I'd always had faith in prayer, but for some reason I'd always had a little more faith in action.

I looked again at some pictures on my phone of Leah and I together. One was a selfie at Santa Monica beach on the day she asked me out. Seeing her beautiful smile and personality made me wonder how anyone could hurt such a soul. Evil had entered our lives.

I walked into the living room and noticed the bracelet Leah had given me on the coffee table. I put it on, and that's when the last memories I had with Leah flooded my mind. The time at the golfing range, eating my last dinner with her and the most striking memory, when I told her, 'I will always be there for you.' There was no way in hell I was going to go against my word. I was a man of my word, especially for Leah and her family.

Something rose up in me—some sort of extra strength or manhood. I decided I would go to the crime scene in the morning and see what happened for myself.

CHAPTER 12

couldn't sleep. I tossed and turned and looked at the clock. I paced and worried. Life was now just a fog of shock and pain. Early in the morning, I hit the freeway for USC. I knew the dorm would be taped off, and the cops wouldn't let me in. I would have to be stealthy.

I listened to the news on the way. They reported a student was missing, a guard had been shot dead, and a police investigation was underway. I hoped and prayed for answers to help us find Leah.

As I drove slowly into the neighborhood, hundreds of students were parking and walking to classes. Police were questioning them. I knew they'd tell me to leave if they knew I wasn't a student. So, I parked my car and walked around the campus perimeter, looking for a way in. I was carrying a sketch I'd drawn from a phone conversation with Leah after she'd moved into her dorm. I'd been on campus once with her after she'd been accepted.

I found a way to enter between some trees and then ducked around a corner, out of sight of police, and found my way to Leah's dorm. LAPD vehicles were parked at the entrance, and cops were standing around talking. Yellow crime tape covered the doors. I hunted for another way in. Then I saw a door! Near it though was a black Suburban with the tailgate open. I didn't see any cops around, so I continued walking to the entrance, my heart pounding. I was scared. I'd never done anything like this before, but considering the circumstances, I figured I had to do whatever it took.

I glanced around, and when I was sure no one was watching, I looked through the small, square window in the door. I didn't see anyone in the hallway or on the stairs, so I went inside. I knew I would only have a few minutes before someone saw me. As soon as I stepped on the first stair, I heard men's voices and footsteps above me, coming down! I hid under the stairs and saw two cops descending. My heart raced. They didn't see me as they walked outside.

Now was my chance. I raced up five flights of stairs, seeing no one on the way but hearing occasional voices. Once I reached the fifth floor, I opened a door that led to a hallway with doors on both sides. Seeing yellow tape in the distance made me sick to my stomach. Shaking, I looked all around me and approached the area slowly. I went under the tape. Then, I stopped in my tracks when I saw a big bloodstain on the carpet. It was all I could do not to heave. I realized it must have been where the security guard was shot.

Making sure not to step on the stain, I continued down the hallway to where I thought Leah's room was. Then I noticed an open door with more yellow tape. I looked both ways, stepped over the tape and began my investigation. I noticed a textbook lying on the floor. A chair and bookcase were knocked over, and knickknacks were scattered, some smashed. A broken frame held a photo of Leah and me. There was glass on the floor. The window was broken, and a breeze was coming in.

As I turned to leave, I noticed Leah's clothes were still there. I was thinking about that when I suddenly got goosebumps all over me. Everything seemed so silent. Surely I hadn't made it in there completely unobserved. My gut told me I was being watched.

I returned to the window, stepped to the side so I wouldn't be seen, and scanned the ground. Everybody was going about their business. No one was looking up. I moved to the middle of the window to get a better view. I searched for anyone hiding behind a tree or a vehicle, but I didn't see anything or anyone unusual. I strained against the sun to get a better view of the tall dorm building across the parking lot. I didn't see anyone looking out any windows. Then, as I looked up, I saw him! On the rooftop was a man with a rifle on a tripod, and it looked like he was pointing it at me! Then I saw his uniform! He was a cop! The rifle looked like it had a suppressor, a drum magazine, and a scope.

A red laser dot showed up on the edge of the window and then moved to my chest—then to my face!

I jumped to the side as the bullet flew into the room and punched into a wall. Two more shots punched through the wall, nearly hitting me and sending drywall dust everywhere!

"Whoa!" I yelled. I threw myself on my stomach. *I don't think he's a cop,* I thought. *Oh, God, he must be one of Javier's cartel men.*

The shooter went from firing semi-auto shots to full auto, and the bullets came flying into the room. Then two cops came running through the doorway. They spread their feet apart, held their handguns at arms' length, and pointed them at me. "Stop right there! Keep your hands where I can see them!"

"Get back!" I yelled. But I was too late. The shooter fired again and killed both men, hitting them multiple times before they fell to the floor.

"Oh God! Oh God!" This was too much for me. Who would protect me if the cops couldn't?

I froze in fear. All I knew was to run for my life. But somehow I had to get the shooter to tell me where Leah was. I peeked around the corner of the window and saw the guy still aiming at me. I darted for the door as more bullets flew at me.

"Son of a bitch!" I yelled as I narrowly dodged the bullets. I ran down the hallway, but the shooter kept firing. Chunks of drywall flew into my face as I sprinted down the hallway. He was firing through the windows in the other dorm rooms that I ran past.

When I got to the staircase, I threw myself against the door. I landed on my face and almost rolled down the stairs. The shots stopped because of the staircase sheltering me from the bullets. I got up and ran downstairs. Two cops stepped in front of me, stopping me in my tracks.

"Hold it right there!" one said, pointing his Glock 19 at me. The other held a Beretta 92F. "Hands behind your head!"

"We have to get out of here!" I panted. "Someone outside is shooting at me!"

"Hands behind your head, and turn around!" one of the cops said as they kept their pointed pistols at me.

"What?" I was stunned that they didn't believe me.

"Hands!" the cop repeated. The other cop grabbed my arm and slammed me into the wall.

"You've got the wrong guy!" I protested.

"Shut up! Keep the hands where we can see them!" One cop frisked me. "What the hell were you doing in that room?"

"I'm not joking! You've got the wrong guy!"

"You got any weapons on you?"

I didn't answer him. I didn't want to waste my time. I wanted to chase the guy who was shooting at me before I lost him.

"Any weapons? Answer me!"

"You guys are making a mistake!"

"Cuff him!" one cop said. "You're under arrest!"

I was desperate to go out and save Leah. I turned around, grabbed the cop by his shirt, and threw him against the concrete wall. He bounced off and fell.

I kicked the pistol out of the other cop's hand. As he tried to punch me, I grabbed his arm, pulled him over and threw him down the stairs. I ran down past him and found him moaning.

"Sorry, dude," I said as I ran out the door.

I charged full speed for the shooter but when I looked up, he was gone! I looked around at the other rooftops but couldn't see him. Then I saw the laser dot moving toward me on the ground! I looked up and saw the guy aiming at me with the dot about to land on my body!

Before the shooter opened fire, I dove behind a Chevy Trailblazer. Bullets ripped through its doors like they weren't even there, punctured its tires, and shattered its windows.

Students screamed and ran for cover. Chunks of pavement flew into my face. I jumped to my feet and sprinted as fast as I could to the building entrance before the shooter could fire at me again. The driver of a Ford F-150 slammed on his brakes and blared his horn as I ran in front of him.

As I neared the entrance, more bullets flew at me, hitting the concrete under my feet. I ran inside and saw a bunch of frightened people huddled together and taking cover.

"Where's the staircase?" I yelled.

"Down the end of the hallway to the left!" one guy yelled back as I ran past.

I raced up five floors, panting, until I found the door to the roof. I pushed it open and came face-to-face with the enemy, who was pointing a Springfield M&P 380 pistol at me. I put my hands in the air as he grinned. "Surprise!"

Then I heard a siren and people yelling from the stairs below. I hoped they were the cops.

"Where's Leah?" I demanded.

"Pretty soon, she'll be everywhere," he said, sneering. "Along with her family. And you're gonna join them."

I knocked the pistol out of his hand and tackled him to the ground. I punched him in the nose until he bled. He grabbed my shirt and threw me off him, sending me rolling on the roof. He pulled out a small knife, but I was still on my back, defenseless. I rolled and grabbed his pistol as he walked over to me, and I sent a 380 bullet straight through his leg.

"Aaaaah!" he screamed as he took another step toward me. I fired another bullet and nicked his leg. He screamed again and began limping backward toward the edge of the roof. I had to catch him before he fell!

"Noooo!" I yelled as I got back on my feet. I charged at him and grabbed him by his shirt. I didn't pull him completely back on the roof. I kept him dangling over the edge so I could negotiate with him and pressed the pistol under his chin.

"Where is she?"

Two police Interceptors charged toward the building, their red-and-blue lights flashing. Several cops ran over on foot. My victim was making choking sounds.

"Tell me where my girlfriend is, and I'll pull you back." The guy didn't say a word. I shook him a little, making him think I was gonna drop him.

"Whoa! Wait!"

"You son of a bitch! I will drop you!"

He still wasn't cooperating with me.

"Tell me!"

I took my eyes off him to look at the cops, and he grabbed my hand, put his thumb over my finger on the trigger, and pushed back. The bullet flew up his chin and straight out the top of his head, and the recoil from the gun caused me to let go of him.

"Nooooo!" I screamed as I tried to catch him, but it was too late. He plummeted to the sidewalk, dead before he hit the ground. I couldn't believe what had happened. The nightmare was getting worse!

"Stay right there!" one cop yelled from the ground.

"Don't move!" another shouted.

I needed to get out of there. I looked around for another way to escape. I saw a huge tree near the building. The cops were charging inside. I backed away about twenty feet from the ledge to get a head start. Then I lunged full-speed ahead. My life depended on it! I jumped as hard as I could toward the tree. The next thing I knew, I was in midair, plunging toward the branches, praying I wouldn't miss. My prayers were answered. I grabbed a branch and swung myself down from branch to branch, like Tarzan.

I was about thirty feet above the ground when a thin branch snapped under my feet, and I fell down the trunk. I landed on my chest against another branch, then on the ground, face down. I got up, spat grass out of my mouth, and quickly brushed the dirt off my clothes.

"There he is!" a cop yelled from the rooftop.

"Don't move!" one cop ordered me.

Yeah right, I thought as I ran away.

"Stop! LAPD!" one cop yelled. "We said stop!"

I had no interest in stopping for those guys. I ran to my GTO and charged out of the campus. Screeching to the exit gate, I smashed through the wooden arm and entered an intersection, blowing through a red light and causing a crash between a Chevy Avalanche and a Ford F-150 crew cab.

I was shocked. I'd walked into a war zone! A dirty cop had fired at me and then killed himself right in front of me—with my finger on the trigger! Now the LAPD was after me. What the hell did Frank get us all into?

CHAPTER 13

didn't know who to trust or what to do.

I drove to Frank and Karen's house, hoping to get an update. I decided not to tell them about what had happened at the campus. It would just rub salt in the wound, scaring them even more.

Frank answered the door. "Josh. Come in." He was holding a red folder with papers in it.

"What's that?"

"These are documents about the court case. I've been trying to figure out what to . . . I haven't made any progress. I've been on the phone all morning with the Justice Department to see if I can get some help. Nothing yet. It's possible they won't even try."

"Your *daughter, my girlfriend,* isn't a good enough reason to try? So that's it? We're on our own with this? So much for our justice system!"

"I know, Josh. I'm doing everything I can. I still have contacts that might help. I know you're scared. I am too. Just hang in there."

"We don't have much time! If we keep relying on your justice system, we're just gonna get more talk, less walk! Look, I know you don't agree with me about that stuff, and I'm sorry, but that's how I feel right now!"

Frank turned his head away.

"Frank, I'm sorry. I didn't mean to get like that with you."

"You're fine," he said. "Why are your clothes so dirty?"

"I . . . um . . . I tripped and fell on my lawn. Where's Karen?"

"Sitting by the pool."

I looked past the living room and saw her. I slid open the glass door and walked up behind her. She was looking at pictures of Leah. Some were recent, and some were older. I put my hand on her shoulder. When she looked at me, her face was misty with tears.

"Hey Josh," she said softly as she took my hand. Then she looked at my clothes, shocked. "What happened to you?"

"Oh, just something stupid," I said. "I tripped and fell on my lawn. How are you doing?"

Karen began to sob. I rubbed her shoulders to comfort her, but I knew it wouldn't help. I knew nothing would comfort me either. "Everything is gonna be OK, Karen."

She looked at me. "How do you know that, Josh? I'm not trying to be rude. I'm just asking what makes you think that? All morning I've been praying for the answer to that."

By that point, even though I believed there was power in prayer, I figured action was just as effective.

"Because I'm here," I said. She looked at me with concern. "That's all you need to know."

I patted her on the shoulder and went back to talk to Frank inside the house.

"You talk to her?" he asked.

"Yeah. She's a mess."

"Listen, Josh, I'm doing everything I can. Try not to worry too much."

"Frank, this is your *daughter* . . . my *girlfriend*. There's nothing that will make me stop worrying."

"I know. All I'm saying is, I'm doing everything I can. Just have faith, and hang in there with me, OK?"

I nodded and then walked away because I didn't want to argue. I went outside to my GTO. feeling useless.

A notification rang on my phone. It was my Bible app telling me the verse of the day, James 4:17: "So whoever knows the right thing to do but fails to do it, for him it is sin." That was not a coincidence. I felt as if God were telling me something.

I wasn't going to sit and wait for Frank to de-escalate the situation. Everybody knew that if you wanted to protect what was yours, you had to protect it yourself. I was a regular citizen with no military, law enforcement, or government background, and I was about to take the law into my own hands. In a world of sheep, lions, and wolves, I decided to be a lion. It felt suicidal, but I was going to fight to save my loved one because that was the right thing to do. I would get my baby back. I decided I wouldn't demand action; I would take action.

I looked back at the house and saw Frank through the window in his office. It occurred to me that his red folder of documents contained information that could help me find Leah. I knew Frank wasn't gonna hand it over to me. I would have to steal it.

Once Frank left his office, I made my move. I climbed through the window, grabbed the folder off his desk, and ran for it.

What was I doing? I was saving Leah.

CHAPTER 14

parked my GTO under Interstate 5, so I was hidden while I reviewed Frank's file. I was looking for Matias's connections, his property and finances—anything I could use against him. I only found his court record, which wasn't going to get me anywhere.

Then I wondered if the information I needed would be inside Frank's computer in his office at the federal building. Getting into his office wouldn't be a walk in the park because it was on the top floor and under strict security. But at that point, I was done playing by the rules.

Sorry, Frank, I thought. *I have to save Leah.*

I raced to my house to get my flash drive to store the information. I left my GTO there and switched to my crotch rocket for a speedy getaway.

The federal building was massive, with a glass exterior. It was connected by a long skywalk to a parking garage on the next block. I parked my motorcycle on the fourth floor and shut off the engine. I took my helmet off and put my black stretch-fit hat on backwards. My hands were shaking.

I joined people heading for the skywalk and went through its sliding glass doors. It looked to be a mile long.

When I made it to the other end, I came to see that getting inside the building was not gonna be as easy as I thought it was going to. I was going to have to go through a security check in before and what made it even hard was I needed a pass card to scan in order for the gate to unlock. Freezing in my tracks, I looked around the lobby for some sort of other way to get in. I came to seeing a guy sitting at table with his brief case sitting on the floor right next to him and his pass card was hanging on the side of his brief case. Since the guy had his back turned on me, it was going to be easy straight forward to steal his card. Quietly walking over to his brief, I unsnapped the card off his brief case and I walked over to the security check in, scanned the card, and walked through the gate as it opened.

I walked down the hallway to the elevator, passing guards and dozens of men who looked like FBI agents in suits and ties, probably with hidden pistols. I kept my head down and made no eye contact.

I made it to the elevator. It was empty. I stepped inside and pushed the button for the top floor. When the doors slid open, I came out to an empty hallway.

I knew Frank's office was at the end because I'd visited him there with Leah once. His door was closed. I started toward it, but suddenly I saw someone open it from the inside! I froze. I could hear people talking inside the office.

Oh no!

I stepped into a utility closet. It was pitch dark inside except for light coming under the door. I heard people walking by. When their footsteps faded, I cracked the door open and was shocked to see Frank with four guards! They walked into the elevator, and the doors closed behind them.

I came out and darted over to Frank's office, where the door had been left open. I went in and closed it. Frank had a corner office with a view overlooking Los Angeles. I hurried past his leather furniture and saltwater fish tank to his cherrywood desk. His computer was on. I plugged the flash drive into the back of the monitor and did my magic.

He had a lot of electronic folders dating back to the early 1990s, so I figured finding the Matias case wouldn't be too difficult. But when I opened it, there was no information in it beyond what I already knew—just the charges and sentencing.

"Ugh. Come on, Frank. I know you have more than that."

I clicked on more files. I couldn't find anything in his emails, documents, or copies of court records. I finally found a folder simply titled "Matias."

"Hmm . . ." I opened it and found out where he'd lived, newspaper articles Frank had collected from one of the lawyers running the case about some criminal cohorts, and other information. I copied it onto my flash drive and then put the drive in my pocket.

Alright, time to bounce.

Before leaving, I opened the desk drawers, on instinct. I was blown away with what I found!

Frank had an LCP 380 ACP pistol and a few extra magazines!

I had to take it. I knew I'd need protection, and I didn't have time to wait for ten days to pass a background check.

"I'm sorry, Frank," I said as I put the weapon and extra magazines in my pocket.

I started for the door, but as I opened it, I froze in terror.

"Who the hell are you?" a security guard asked.

"Um . . . maintenance. Here to dust the furniture."

He showed me his badge. "You need to come with us."

I slammed the door in his face and locked it.

"Hey! Hey!" he yelled. "Open this door!"

Oh, God, what do I do? I grabbed a chair and put the back of it between the doorknob and floor.

"Who's in there?" I heard Frank's ask.

"Some kid. He locked himself in your office."

"Here, I'll unlock the door," Frank said.

Now I was panicking even more because I was cornered in Frank's office with no way of escaping.

He unlocked the door, but the chair kept it closed. They started banging and kicking it.

"Open the door!" one of the men yelled.

I ran over to the window. It was a straight drop to the ground, but over to the left, three floors below me, was a large balcony. If I could get onto it, I could run back inside the building and make my escape. I hatched a plan. I could bust open Frank's window, tie his drapes together, and use them to swing over to the balcony, like George of the Jungle.

Usually heights didn't bother me, but this was ridiculous. I was scared, but it was the only idea I had. How would I break his window though? It was safety glass. I'd need a sledgehammer to break it. The heaviest thing I could find was a chair.

The guards were banging on the door, and judging by the way the chair under the doorknob was bouncing around, I didn't have a lot of time.

I grabbed the other chair by the back legs and swung it at the window. On the third swing, a long crack formed from top to bottom. After two more swings, the window finally shattered. I ripped the curtains off the rods and knotted them together. Then I tied one end to the air conditioner below the window and threw the other end outside.

I can't believe I'm doing this.

The men were still banging on the door, and the chair had moved slightly out from under the knob. It was time for me to face my fear. I grabbed the curtain with both hands and climbed out onto the ledge. Just then the chair holding the door slipped, and the guards kicked their way in. The door almost flew off its hinges.

"Hold it right there!" one of them yelled, pointing his pistol at me.

My foot slipped off the ledge, and I fell to the end of the drapes. I gripped them so hard that I nearly burned my skin off. My heart pounded.

Oh God! This is not good!

I looked up at the window and saw three guards staring down at me.

"Don't move! We're coming to get you!"

I started using my feet to push myself left and right and swing out from the building, so I could get some momentum.

"Don't move! We're bringing you up!"

I kept swinging. After a minute or two, I swung way out toward the balcony, let go of the drapes, and threw myself toward it. I was just able to grab the edge by the tips of my fingers. Sweating and groaning, I pulled myself up.

"Stop!" a guard yelled.

"I ain't stopping for you, badge boy," I muttered under my breath.

I ran through some double doors, through another office, through another door, and down a hallway. The elevator doors slid open. I pushed the button for the fourth floor, and the elevator started moving down but not fast enough.

"Oh, come on, come on, come on!"

When I was halfway down, I heard a security alarm.

"Oh, great. Just what I need."

A few seconds later, the elevator stopped, the doors slid open, and I ran down the hallway.

"Over there!" a guy yelled. I turned around and saw ten guards about sixty feet from me, running toward me with pistols. I sprinted to the skywalk and ran past everyone on it. When I got to the parking garage, I realized my motorcycle wasn't close enough to reach before they could grab me.

I saw a black SUV coming toward me with some old dude driving it. I took out my LCP pistol and pointed it at him.

"Stop!"

He slammed on the brakes, with a look of shock.

"Out of the car!"

I started toward the driver's door while he raised his hands. I opened the door, keeping the pistol pointed at him.

"I'm not gonna hurt you," I said. "I just need to borrow your car. Now get out!" He got out, and I got in.

"You picked the wrong place to steal a car, kid," the guy said.

I shifted into drive.

"I'm not stealing it." I turned the steering wheel toward the skywalk entrance, hit the gas, drove the SUV straight through the sliding glass doors, and parked it so that it blocked the entrance.

"You son of a bitch!" the old man yelled.

I jumped out and ran full speed for my motorcycle.

"Sorry!" I called back over my shoulder.

I made it to my motorcycle, grabbed my helmet, and jumped on.

I looked back and saw some guards on their radios, probably calling for backup. I had to get outta that garage! I rode off the fourth floor, down to the third and the second. When I made it to the bottom and was racing toward the toll booth, two guards stepped out, pointing their pistols at me.

"Stop right there!" one yelled. I should have done just that. Instead, I opened the throttle and flew right past them, nearly clipping one of them in his arm. I broke through the gate arm and spun onto the busy street, nearly hitting the side of a FedEx truck. I raced down the streets of Los Angeles, until I was miles away.

God, Almighty. What have I just done? If Frank knew I'd been in his office, he'd kill me. But all I could think of was saving Leah.

CHAPTER 15

raced back to my house, grabbed my laptop, plugged in the flash drive, and began going through Frank's files. I saw a picture of Alonso Matias, a clean-cut Latino with short brown hair and brown eyes. He was the same height as me, five feet eight inches, but more muscular. He was fifty-five, born in Cancun into a Mexican cartel family operating in Nort h and South America. His US rap sheet showed he'd been involved in drug trafficking, money laundering, and other offenses. Frank also had copies of Mexican newspaper accounts describing how every person who had ever arrested anyone in the Matias family, testified against them, or been a judge or part of a jury involved in his case had gone missing.

One article had a picture of another Latino man: Juan Garcia, fifty, bald, with a brown goatee, green eyes, 6 foot 6 inches, 250 pounds, with python-sized arms. According to the article, he was Alonso Matias's brother, and he was Alonso's main bodyguard. Juan was an ex-Marine in the Mexican special forces, specializing in close encounters, demolitions and weapons handling. The guy was a born killer. He had been charged with war crimes and sent to prison but was release with Alonso's help of course.

One story noted that the family owned some Los Angeles

businesses and had connections with one of the biggest banks in the United States. They also had a big hand in US oil fields, freighters, and political offices. This stuff was beyond me, but it looked like they were working in conjunction with the mafia. The cartel had been funding everything from oil and gas to weapons and drugs. Worst of all, their money and connections made them untouchable.

"This is gonna be harder than I thought," I groaned.

Then something caught my eye. The family owned a Mercedes Benz dealership in Beverly Hills.

Well, well, what do we have here? I thought. I knew that dealership. The general manager was Raul Ortega. According to a note in Frank's file, the FBI was investigating whether Ortega had been laundering money for the cartel. I wondered if I should have a chat with Ortega. Maybe he had information that could help me find Leah.

I couldn't believe Frank had become involved in this. These people weren't the usual psychopaths off the street. This was heavy information.

Can my life be any worse than it is right now? I wondered.

I turned on the TV news to see what they were reporting on Leah's case.

"The USC campus has been on high alert for the past two days," a Fox News anchor said. "Yesterday, a security guard was found shot to death in the hallway of a dorm building. Today, the school reported a shooting spree that left three police officers dead. A suspect was seen fleeing the scene in a black car soon after the shots were fired. Authorities were able to identify him from street cameras as he was driving away."

Then they showed my driver's license photo and the street surveillance of me driving out the college. "The LAPD and the FBI are asking the public for any information about the whereabouts of the suspect, twenty-five-year-old Joshua Daniels. Here you can see his picture. He has brown eyes and light-brown hair. He's clean shaven and is about five fee eight inches. One of our reporters is on the scene with more details about the incident."

"Thank you," the reporter said. "Behind the yellow tape, you can see the FBI forensics team and the coroner's staff working this scene. We spoke to one of the police officers who saw the entire event this morning. He and his partner were involved in an altercation with the suspect in the dorm building staircase. They later found two officers dead in the building. The officer told me the suspect shot a third officer and threw his body off the roof of another dorm building. This is what the officer had to say."

The reporter cut to a clip of the cop talking. I recognized him instantly from fighting him in the staircase.

"My partner and I heard shots being fired, so we ran upstairs and came face to face with the suspect."

"Did he say anything to you?" the reporter asked.

"He said, 'Get out of my way. You got the wrong guy.' When we tried to cuff him, he attacked us. We chased him, and we saw him up on the roof of a different building, pointing a gun at another officer. He shot him point blank and then threw the officer over the roof. Unfortunately, he was able to escape, jumping down that tree over there, and he took off in another vehicle."

The scene cut back to the reporter.

"Joshua Daniels is believed to be armed and extremely dangerous. If you see him, notify the LAPD immediately."

I turned to other networks. I was on CNN, MSNBC, CBS, ABC, and independent media on the Internet. *What must Leah's family be thinking? What are our friends thinking?* I decided I couldn't worry about that, as much as the thought haunted me.

My phone rang. I thought it would be Alonso, but it was Frank.

I let it go to voicemail. I knew he'd be pissed as hell, and I needed a few seconds to think. Then I picked up the voicemail.

"Josh! I just saw you on the news for killing three police officers. What the hell is going on? I told you *not* to do anything rash, and now this! My daughter's been kidnapped, and now Karen and I have to deal with this! Josh, I . . . None of this is making sense! This doesn't sound like you. Call me right now! I mean it!"

I didn't have time to argue with Frank. I felt bad for trashing his office and embarrassing him. That was not part of my plan, but I had to do what was needed to get out of there. The clock was ticking. I needed to do whatever was necessary. I'd have to talk to Frank when this was all over. For now, I had to find Leah before it was too late.

As I walked back into the garage for motorcycle, I realized the pistol was the only weapon I had. I needed some kind of backup in case anything happened. I grabbed a spring-loaded pocket knife out of my tool chest, which was perfect for up-close encounters.

CHAPTER 16

The Mercedes Benz dealership was a huge, glass-sided building. I parked my motorcycle at the entrance just in case I had to make a run for it again. I had the LCP pistol in my hoodie pocket and my pocketknife in my jeans.

I walked into the showroom where about ten brand-new cars and SUVs were on display. Salesmen were talking to customers. I walked up to the young receptionist, who smiled at me.

"Hello! Can I help you?"

"I'm here to see Raul Ortega."

"I'll page him for you. Do you have an appointment?"

"Yeah. Appointment."

She called him. "Mr. Ortega? There's a young man here to see . . . OK." She took the phone off her ear and put it on her shoulder. "I'm sorry, but he's a little busy right now."

"It can't wait," I said. "It's . . . important."

She looked at me with concern, then put the phone back on her ear. "Um, sir, he said it can't wait. It has to be now."

I heard a click on the other end. The woman hung up. "So, um, you planning on buying a car?" she asked.

"Not exactly." However, I did have a plan that involved the LCP, my pocket knife, and torture. I didn't plan on killing Ortega. I just wanted to get him to talk.

He came out of his office in his expensive black suit. "What's so important?" he asked. Then he looked at me, shocked. He knew who I was and why I was there to see him.

"Hello, Mr. Ortega," I said. "I need a minute, if you don't mind."

Ortega and the woman looked at each other, and then he looked at me.

"This way sir," he said. He started for his office, and I followed him. He pulled out his phone and started texting. When we entered his office, I shut the door and locked it, then shut the blinds. Ortega walked behind his desk, put his phone down, and opened a drawer.

My heart raced, as he reached for a Walther PPK pistol. As he tried to draw it, I grabbed his wrist and punched his nose, then grabbed the back of his head and slammed his face into the desk. I kept his head pinned down while holding his wrist.

"Drop it," I said quietly.

Ortega dropped the pistol onto the floor, and I released his wrist. Then I grabbed my phone and put its screen, which had a picture of Leah on it, up to his face.

"I'm looking for this girl. Where is she?"

"Who the hell are you?"

I slammed his head into the desk again and kept my phone in his face. "You know who I am. And guess what? I know who you are too. I know everything about you, Ortega. The owner of this dealership kidnapped my girlfriend. I'm pretty sure you know about that."

"I don't know what you're talking about," Ortega said.

I put my phone in my pocket and grabbed the LCP.

"Oh, really? Let's see if I can jog your memory." I pointed my pistol into the side of his head.

"Whoa—whoa! OK! Wait a second! Wait! OK! I . . . I know who she is."

"Yeah, I figured. I wanna know *where* she is."

"I don't know!" Ortega said. "Look, kid, Alonso doesn't tell me a lot about his business outside of the dealership. He told me about your girlfriend, yes, but he didn't mention where she was being held."

"Stop lying!"

"I'm not!"

"Are you gonna talk, or are you gonna test the extremely low amount of patience I have right now?"

"I have no idea where she is! Do I look like the person who kidnapped your girlfriend? I'm just the GM of the dealership!"

He was lying. So, I stepped things up. Keeping the pistol against his head, I grabbed my pocketknife, released the spring-loaded blade, and stabbed Ortega's hand. Blood gushed out of the top and bottom of his hand, all over the desk.

"Aaaah-aaaaah!" he screamed. I pressed my hand over his mouth.

"Here's what I'm gonna do. I'm going to cut clean through your hand, all the way up to your arm, cutting your hand in half." He continued moaning and screaming as I began cutting farther up his hand. "And I will keep cutting until one of two things happens: you tell me what I want to know, or you bleed to death."

I cut an inch farther up his hand, grinding against bone.

He moaned in agony.

"Gee, that didn't sound good. Does that hurt?" I asked.

Ortega's face was bright red, and he was sweating. Tears were pouring out of his eyes.

I cut another inch. "Just imagine the pain when I cut your hand in half."

"Aaaah!" Ortega screamed under my hand. Then he began trying to talk. Just then he got a text message.

"Who the hell is that?" I asked.

I picked up the phone and found that Alonso had sent Ortega a message. Ortega's first text to Alonso read, "The kid's at the dealership! Where are you?" Alonso's response said, "Five minutes."

That scared the hell out of me. He was coming!

Ortega elbowed me in the side of my face and shoved me off my feet. I landed on the floor, dropping my pistol.

He pulled the knife out of his blood-covered hand, dropped it on the floor, and then picked up his Walther PPK.

"You're not gonna find your girlfriend," he said, sneering. "She's gonna die." He cocked his pistol. "And you know what? So are you."

I leaped to my feet and tackled him with both my arms wrapped around his waist. We rolled over his desk, knocking everything off, including his computer. Then I grabbed his hand that held the pistol and took hold of his throat, trying to choke him. I banged his pistol hand against the floor, trying to knock the weapon out of his grasp. Instead, the impact of his hand hitting the floor made his finger pull the trigger, and the gun went off! The bullet shattered the window, and the people in the showroom started screaming.

I grabbed the weapon. Ortega shoved me, and I fell onto my back. He crawled on top of me, holding my arm down. Then he grabbed the pistol. While he had a grip on it, I pulled the trigger, and the slide pinched his thumb inside the chamber.

"Aaaaaah!" he screamed as blood gushed out of his thumb.

I released the pistol and pushed Ortega off me. He landed flat on his back, the pistol still locked on his thumb.

As I reached for my pistol on the floor, Ortega pulled his gun off his thumb. Before he could point it at me, I grabbed my LCP and fired two shots into his chest. Blood splattered everywhere, and he fell against the wall and slid to the floor. He heaved, struggling for air, his Walther PPK still in his hand. He tried to point it at me.

I kept my LCP trained on Ortega. "Don't do it!" I said, but Ortega kept raising his pistol at me. "Don't make me do it!" I yelled, but he left me no choice. I fired another shot into his chest. He dropped the gun, his head slumped forward, and his body fell sideways. Blood ran out of his mouth. I walked over to him. He wasn't breathing. I checked his pulse. He was dead.

I couldn't believe I'd just killed someone. I felt faint, and I began to shake uncontrollably. *What would happen to me now? I didn't even get any answers out of him.*

Then a single thought coursed through my mind: *I have to get out of here!*

I stormed out of his office and headed for an exit.

When the receptionist saw Ortega dead on the floor, she started screaming.

I froze when I saw two Ford F-150 crew cabs and a Lincoln Navigator pulling into the parking lot. Eight men got out, and I recognized two of them—Alonso and Juan!

I thought the scary part was seeing every one of those guys carrying machine guns, but when Juan opened the rear of the Navigator, he grabbed an M249 SAW that was belt fed to the back pack that he put on after he grabbed the weapon. I stood in the showroom, frozen with fear. I didn't know where to hide.

Juan walked toward the dealership and pointed the weapon at the front entrance—right where I was standing.

"Everyone get down!" I screamed. Juan pulled the trigger, firing through the glass at about twenty bullets per second. Shards of glass and pieces of cars flew everywhere as people screamed and ducked for cover.

I hit the floor and crawled behind an SUV.

"Son of a bitch!" I yelled as I lay on my stomach. Bullets punched through the SUV, shattering the windows and doors and shredding the tires. I was too scared to move.

After thirty seconds, they stopped shooting.

I got up on my knees, leaned against the back of the SUV, and peeked around the corner. Everything inside the showroom was destroyed.

I saw Juan put down his weapon and pull out a Desert Eagle .50 caliber pistol from his holster. Then he and Alonso and the other men made their way into the showroom.

I was outnumbered ten to one, and all I had was my pistol. I had to react quickly. I knew it was another crazy idea, but I thought about my motorcycle parked right at the corner of the showroom entrance. If I could get to it without getting shot, I could ride it through the showroom, break through the doors, and haul it out of the dealership, taking the other exit of the parking lot.

I got to my feet and ran through the debris toward my bike.

"There's Daniels!" one of the men outside yelled. They fired their machine guns at me. Bullets flew, hitting the wall behind me. As I got closer to the glass door, I pulled out my pistol, fired four shots at it, and shattered the glass. I ran through the open doorway, hopped on my crotch rocket, fired up the engine, opened the throttle wide, screeching the rear tire, and shot through the doorway, into the showroom.

"Take him out!" one of the men yelled. They fired their machine guns at me as I raced through the showroom. As bullets flew past me, I felt like I was some kind of action hero.

Then, reality hit me in the face. One of the men surprised me at the door with his G36C rifle. I slammed my front brake, making the bike do a stoppie with the back wheel in the air. Then I turned the front wheel to the left, spun the bike around, and used the back wheel to knock the man off his feet. He flipped sideways and landed hard on the floor.

Once I landed the back wheel on the floor, I hit the throttle and rode straight through the double glass doors, speeding away from the dealership as Juan fired at me. I swerved onto the busy street, nearly hitting the side of a dump truck, and sped off.

CHAPTER 17

parked my motorcycle in my garage and then went straight into the kitchen. I stood over the sink, feeling like I was about to throw up. I couldn't believe I had actually killed someone, taken a life. I turned on the faucet, put my head in the sink, and let loose, puking out everything I had in my stomach until I was weak. I heaved and coughed, trying to get air.

I backed away from the sink until I hit the other counter, then slid down onto the floor.

"Oh, Lord! Oh, Lord" I said. I couldn't hold it back any longer. I covered my face with my hands and burst into tears.

Until I pulled the trigger on Ortega, I hadn't known what death was. It was scary to see, especially because I caused it. I needed comfort, but I had no one to give me that. I didn't even feel the Lord's presence. I felt so alone physically and spiritually no matter how much I prayed.

After a few minutes of sitting on the floor, I settled down, took my hands off my face, and looked up at the ceiling, hoping to find some sort of answer from God. Ever since Leah was kidnapped, it seemed like God had gone silent and left me on my own.

My phone rang. I grabbed it and saw Karen on the caller ID.

I really wanted to answer her, but I didn't. I figured she might be giving me an angry call the way Frank had. I let it go to voicemail. Then I listened to the message. She sounded emotional.

"Josh? Please call me. I'm so scared right now. Frank and I saw the news earlier, and they're saying all these crazy things about you killing cops. I don't want to believe it because that doesn't sound like you at all. It doesn't make any sense. Josh . . . just please call me. Don't call Frank because he's madder than hell right now. Call me, OK? We love you, Josh! Please be safe."

I thought that maybe I should've answered her call because at least she was coming at me in a nicer way than Frank.

While I tried to figure out what to do next, I decided to put gas in my car.

I pulled into a station, parked at a pump, ran my card through the machine and got back in the car while the tank filled. I took a long, deep breath and leaned against the headrest, hoping no one at the crowded station would recognize me. My fear for Leah was making my blood pressure go through the roof, and my heart felt like it was about to burst out of my chest.

I pulled out my phone and started scrolling through pictures of Leah from social media. Some photos showed us together. Leah loved to take pictures and videos of us together with funny filters and voices. We did funny TikTok videos together, which was always fun. It's good for the soul to laugh at yourself.

As I thought about my life, I realized Leah and her parents were the only family I'd ever had. I wasn't in contact with any of my relatives, and I didn't have a lot of friends. If Leah lost her life, my heart would break, and I'd probably never heal. I began to sob. I looked up at the sky. I wanted to talk to God, but I didn't know what to say. Would He even listen?

I reflected on when I first met Leah. It was the start of a beautiful journey.

Five years earlier I was sitting at a table by myself at a Starbucks studying for my final exam on my laptop.

As I concentrated on my work, one of the baristas came up to me with a mocha in her hand. "Excuse me, sir. This is for you," she said as he put the drink in front of me.

"Um . . . I didn't order that," I replied.

"I know. It's from one of those young ladies over there," the barista said and then walked off.

I looked at the cup, which had a note written on it. It said "Hi! The girl in the brown leather jacket."

I looked up to see a group of girls. Then I spotted the girl who had sent me the mocha. It was Leah, and it was love at first sight, which I never really believed in. But the first sight of Leah made me rethink that.

I got out of my chair and started toward Leah, mocha in hand. When the girls saw me approaching, they got quiet, and a couple of them giggled.

Once I reached up to Leah, I stood there for a moment grinning as I tried to figure out what to say.

"Um . . . Hi," I said. Leah didn't say anything. Instead, she looked at her girlfriends and giggled. Something about her giggle made her even more attractive. It was cute.

Leah stood up. "Hi. I'm Leah," she said, and then we shook hands.

"Josh," I replied. "So, um . . . would you like to join me at my table?"

Leah smiled at me. "Yeah, sure."

We talked for hours that day getting to know each other.

I started going to Leah's church after she invited me. One night, Leah and I were walking out of a Bible study when we decided to take a walk on Santa Monica Pier. It was eight o'clock and the sun was just setting. The pier was quiet. It was just Leah and me walking with our sodas, holding hands. and talking.

"You know, Josh, I really enjoy being with you," she said.

"I enjoy being with you too."

She told me that she felt safe with me everywhere we went. "It's like I have nothing to worry about, you know?"

I told her I wanted her to feel safe. "It's what BFFs do," I said. "They look after each other."

She pulled me next to her. "Hey, Josh, I've had something on my mind . . . about you and me and our friendship."

"Do you like our friendship?" I asked.

"Of course I do. I love that you're my best friend, but lately after hanging out with you, I actually . . . Josh, how do you feel about having a girlfriend?"

"A girlfriend? Leah? Are you asking me if I want to be in a relationship with you?"

Leah locked her eyes on mine, smiling. "Yeah, I guess I am. I'm sorry, Josh. I'm not pressuring you, am I?"

"No, no, no, not at all." I couldn't believe my good fortune. I smiled. "Leah, I . . . I'd love to be your boyfriend."

She gave me the biggest smile and then threw her arms around my neck. I put my arms around her back. I figured I'd just landed me a nice fish.

Sometime later, Leah and I were at an outdoor ice-skating rink, crowded with people. It was freezing. It was Leah's first time skating, so I was teaching her how to move around, holding onto the rail. She was struggling to keep her balance, but I wasn't going to let her fall.

"Ooooooh! Whoa!" she cried as she almost fell backwards. "This is harder than it looks!"

"You're doing OK," I said. "Just keep your balance, and move your legs. Use your skates to move forward." She began to glide and move a little faster. It looked as if she didn't need me. "You think you're good without me holding on?" I asked.

"I'll try," she said. I released her hand, and she started gliding, but when she tried to do longer stretches, she began to lose her balance and fall backwards. I rushed over and caught her.

"Whoa!" she exclaimed.

"I got you. I got you. I'm not gonna let you fall."

She turned to face me. We were kissing distance from each other. "I've got you," I said, smiling. She beamed at me, looking into my eyes. "I got you," I repeated. We chuckled. "Now, try again."

She started moving around the rink alongside me until she was able to do it on her own.

"There you go!" I shouted.

She steered into my arms and came within kissing distance again, looking into my eyes.

"I'll never let you fall," I repeated. "I'll always be there to catch you." Then Leah slowly moved her lips toward mine, and I experienced the most magical moment I'd ever experienced in my life. She put her arms around my neck and kissed my lips with her blueberry lip gloss. I put my arms around her back and let her kiss me for as long as she wanted. "I don't feel so cold anymore," she whispered. "Do you?"

I shook my head, looking into her eyes. "I'm burning up," I said quietly. Leah kissed me again, and we held each other, kissing right in the middle of the rink while everyone skated around us. That moment was so dreamlike that it felt like everyone around us disappeared, and it was just Leah and me.

As I reminisced, still sitting in the car at the gas station, I also thought of our one-year anniversary at the Olive Garden restaurant.

"Happy anniversary, Leah," I said.

"Happy anniversary, Josh," she replied, and we clinked glasses. She put hers down and then picked up a string of pasta and put one end of it in her mouth. She handed me the other end, so we could do the *Lady and the Tramp* spaghetti kiss. After we kissed at the end of the noodle, we laughed. Relationship goals for sure.

"I've always wanted to do that," she said.

"I think every couple wants to do that at least once," I mused.

Leah grinned. "You're the only person I can ever be silly with." Suddenly, her face became serious. "Josh . . . I love you."

I was so shocked that I didn't know how to respond. I'd never been told that before. I looked away and didn't say anything.

"Josh? Josh? Did you hear me?"

"I . . . heard," I said, avoiding eye contact.

"Josh?" Leah got up out of her chair, ready to walk over to me. "Josh . . . ?"

"Sit back down," I said quietly. Leah returned to her seat, surprised.

"Josh, I'm sorry."

"Leah, listen to me. What you said . . . nobody has ever said that to me before. You have no idea how happy that made me feel." We smiled at each other. I felt tears welling up in me. I knew she saw them. "I love you too, Leah. And I always will."

Leah got up and walked to me, I stood up, and we hugged and kissed.

I let out a deep sigh as I pondered the sweet memory. Then I said a quick prayer, hoping God could hear my heavy heart. "Lord . . . I know I don't talk to you as much as I should. You always say that You are love, that You feel my pain, that You know my weaknesses and strengths. Well, I'm afraid. I know I don't deserve anything from You. I don't deserve Your love because of all the hatred I've thrown at You over the years, but Leah loves You, and she needs your protection. She's the greatest person You've brought into my life. My parents didn't want me, and none of my relatives wanted contact with me. I don't have a very big social life, but You gave me Leah and her parents, and that's all I need in this world. I need You, and I need them. Just please help me . . . please . . . please." I wiped the tears off my face.

I heaved a sigh and then shut my eyes for a bit, trying to get a least of little bit of relaxation.

Then I heard a car approaching from behind. When I opened my eyes, I looked in my rear-view mirror, and my stress returned! Two cops in a Ford Explorer Interceptor had pulled up! What if they were dirty cops on Alonso's payroll? What if they were clean cops who were looking for me? Either way, I was screwed.

One got out and started pushing buttons on the pumps. Both men had their eyes on me. I raised my hoodie over my head and slid down into my seat.

A few seconds later, my gas nozzle clicked, but I didn't get out of my car right away. They both still had their eyes locked on me like they were waiting for me to get out. The feeling made my skin crawl.

Finally, I got out of my car, leaving the door open, and kept my hoodie over my head. I hung the nozzle on the pump. When I was about to get back in my car, when one of the cops called to me.

"Excuse me, sir?"

I froze, my back to them. The cop inside the vehicle got out and stood beside the door while the other one walked toward me.

I turned slightly toward him. He looked me up and down, and I noticed he had his hand on his pistol.

"The tint on your windows and front windshield are way too dark," he said. "You can't have them darker than seventy-five percent."

"I'll get it removed," I said. "Well, have a good day." As I was about to get back in my car, the cop shut the door on me and pulled out another weapon he had hidden behind him beneath his shirt: a full-auto Micro Uzi. He jabbed it into my spleen and grabbed my arm.

My heart started pounding again. I sighed and rolled my eyes. Just as I'd thought, they were working for Alonso.

The cop pulled my hoodie down.

"Here's what's up," the cop said quietly. "I'm gonna put you in cuffs, walk you to the back of my Interceptor, and then I'm gonna make sure you are never seen or heard from again. Put your hands behind your back."

Rather than cooperate, I just stood there looking at the ground, my heart pounding.

"Don't test me, kid. You're being watched by more than just me and my partner over there. You're not going anywhere now."

I saw two more vehicles in a parking lot next to the gas station, a Dodge Durango SRT Hellcat and another Ford Explorer Interceptor. Both had multiple guys inside looking at me.

"We can do this one of two ways," the cop said. "One, we take you quietly, and everyone else lives, or two, I'll kill you right here and then we'll kill everyone else at this station."

I looked around and saw people at every pump. Some had their families with them. Like hell I was going to let these dirty cops kill these innocent people.

"Your choice," the cop said.

I looked him straight in the eye. "I think I'll go with the third option," I said quietly. "I kill you, and everyone else lives."

I grabbed the Uzi, punched him in his face, and restrained him by twisting his arm until he lost control of the weapon.

The other cop drew his pistol, so I turned my cop's hand to

point the Uzi at his partner and fired. The guy ran and hid behind the Interceptor as bullets flew. People screamed and hid. Children were crying.

The cop tried to point the Uzi at me, but I kicked his kneecap, almost breaking it. He moaned and grabbed his knee while I got control of his weapon. I moved his wrist, pointed the Uzi at his foot, and fired three shots into his shoe.

"Aaaaaaaaaah!" He screamed. He got down on one knee. I still had both hands on his wrist. I grabbed his arm while keeping my hand on his wrist and I twisted until I heard his arm crack—twice. He howled in pain and dropped the weapon. I grabbed it and fired into his chest until the magazine was empty, and he fell to the ground, dying in a pool of blood.

Now, I had to get rid of the other cop. I tossed the Uzi away and grabbed my pistol from my car. The officer appeared from behind the Interceptor with a Remington 870 shotgun, so I ran and hid behind a minivan. He fired a shot at me and it punched right through the van. I found a man and woman hiding there too. The woman began to scream.

"Get out of here! Go!" I yelled and they ran inside the gas station.

The cop fired two more shots, and the bullets shattered the minivan's windows. I fired through the van, and it nicked the side of the cop's leg.

"Gaaaa!" he screamed as blood gushed out of his leg. He limped and hid on the driver's side of the Interceptor. I started firing my pistol into it. He fired again, and his bullets punched right through the minivan.

"Son of a bitch!" I yelled as I ran from the hail of bullets. I jumped and rolled over the hood of a Range Rover Sport and hid beside it.

When the cop stopped shooting, I peeked over the Rover's hood and pointed my pistol at him, but he took cover again by the vehicle. I fired and shattered the headlight. My pistol was empty!

"Damn it!" I said as I hid beside the Rover and slammed in another magazine. Three more shots shattered the windows right above me, and glass landed on my head.

I heard footsteps limping over to me. I peeked beneath the Rover and saw him limping toward me.

I lay on my side on the concrete, pointed my pistol at his leg, and pulled the trigger. The bullet hit his leg and pierced it.

"Gaaaaaaaaah!" he screamed. He dropped his shotgun and went down on his knees, his leg bleeding profusely, and covered the wound with both hands.

Then I did the darkest thing I've ever done. As I made my way toward the cop, I put my pistol in my jeans pocket and grabbed the cop's shotgun off the ground. Once I came face to face with him, the cop looked up at me, and I pointed the shotgun right into his face. He looked shocked as I pulled the trigger.

The Dodge Durango and the Interceptor pulled out of the other parking lot and sped toward me. When they were thirty feet from me when I pointed the shotgun at the Interceptor's windshield and fired. Both vehicles stopped dead, and the cops ducked under the dashboards. The driver of the Interceptor shifted into reverse and hit the gas, screeching the front tires, and then sped away as I kept firing at them. The vehicle swerved, then slammed into the side of a parked Nissan Pathfinder.

When the shotgun emptied, I grabbed my pistol and pointed it at the Durango. When I was about to pull the trigger, I saw someone I recognized riding shotgun! My jaw dropped. It was Detective Davis! I couldn't believe it! I was so angry, I opened fire.

"Move back!" Davis yelled. He and the other men ducked under the dash, but I kept firing. The driver started backing up, screeching the rear tires. I fired until my pistol was empty, but I didn't hit any of them.

I ran back to my car, threw my pistol in the console, then fired up the engine and screeched out of the station.

The cops chased me, the Interceptor's red-and-blue LED lights flashing. I was so amped up, I nearly hit a Ford Mustang head on. The driver blared his horn, spun, and drove into the curb.

As the Interceptor roared up behind me, I shifted into sixth gear and careened down a 35 mph zone on a double-lane road doing over 60 mph. Ahead was a busy intersection, and the light was red.

Oh God, I thought. But I couldn't let that stop me. The traffic was jammed for a long way. I would have to turn into oncoming traffic and dodge cars, so I maneuvered into the lane and zig-zagged among the vehicles, the Durango and Interceptor still in hot pursuit.

An SUV slid into the curb. Then I nearly sideswiped another vehicle. I charged into the intersection. Before I made it completely through, a pickup trying to avoid me turned and slammed head on into a sedan and flipped right in front of me!

I hoped the accident would block the Durango and the Interceptor, but they maneuvered around it and kept coming at me.

I wasn't going to lose them in the busy streets of LA, so I took the entry ramp to westbound Interstate 105 and immersed myself into six lanes of traffic. The men kept up with me without a problem, however. The Durango came right up to my bumper, rear-ending and damaging my GTO.

He did it again, and after that, a passenger stood up through the sunroof with a FN P90 submachine gun. He fired into the back of my car, leaving holes in my trunk and shattering the taillights and back window.

"Son of a bitch!" I yelled. I punched the gas pedal to the floor and steered into the far-right lane while the Durango stayed in the middle lane, and the guy kept firing at me.

Eventually, he stopped shooting and crawled back inside the Durango. I thought he was done, but I was wrong because he shortly came out with an M72 anti-tank rocket launcher!

"Oh hell no!" I said. I floored the gas, overtaking three pickup trucks and a semi-truck towing a flatbed trailer with a large Bobcat front-end loader on it. I stayed on the side of the semi-truck, but that didn't stop the cop from firing the rocket launcher. It hit the semi-truck's receiver hitch, and then a massive fiery explosion erupted between the tractor and trailer, causing them to separate. A small piece of debris from the tractor smashed through my window and hit the side of my head, slicing my face.

I looked in the rear-view mirror and watched the tractor roll onto its side, and then the whole semi-truck flipped toward me. The front-end loader broke loose and landed in front of my car. I swerved and narrowly missed a major accident. When I looked in my rear-view mirror, I saw a pickup trying to avoid the front-end loader. It slammed into the edge of the scoop, flipped on its side, and barrel-rolled down the highway.

Still, the men chased me. The guy who fired the rocket launcher climbed back inside the Durango.

Ahead, I saw a traffic jam across all six lanes, then a paving crew beyond that, working in all but one lane. I steered into the far-right lane, the Durango and Interceptor still right behind me.

I passed all the stationary vehicles and came to a parked semi that was blocking the emergency lane. I steered around it and hit some orange barrels, then screeched into the middle of the construction, going from the pavement to a dirt road. The workers ran for cover.

Out of nowhere, a black 2006 Ram 1500 mega cab pulled out

in front of me. I swerved around it, barely missing the front end. It screeched to a halt, and I flew past it, the Durango and Interceptor right behind me.

As I hit the dirt road, my tires created a big cloud of dust. I hoped it would blind my pursuers, causing them to crash. I slowed down slightly until the Interceptor came close to my bumper. Then I punched the gas to the floor. My rear tires spun, digging up dirt and gravel.

Now that there was a big distance between me and the Interceptor, I looked for something ahead for the Interceptor to run into. I saw a front-end loader with forklift forks on it. Even better, the forks were facing us, and they were at a perfect height to pierce the Interceptor's cab.

I drove straight toward the loader, then hard-steered away at the last second. The Interceptor slammed right into the forks, which smashed through the windshield and killed the cops!

That was a huge relief. I was dripping in sweat and covered in dirt, my face bleeding. One vehicle down. I still had to get rid of the Durango. I decided to blow out one of its front tires and cause a crash.

I slowed down until it came to my bumper. Then I grabbed my pistol.

Oh Lord, please let this work, I prayed.

The Durango repeatedly rear-ended me.

I held the pistol in my left hand, ready to fire. My right hand held the steering wheel, preparing to do a hard turn. I braced myself for about ten seconds. Then I hit the clutch and the brakes, turned the steering wheel hard left, and spun to the side of the Durango. I pointed the pistol at the driver's-side tire, fired two shots, and missed. On the third shot though, the bullet pierced it. The tire exploded, and the Durango careened past me and up and over a large pile of dirt. It flew into the air and landed on top of a GMC Sierra 1500, then barrel-rolled onto the ground and into the side of a cement truck.

I wondered if Davis or any of the other guys survived. I didn't think they did because they hit the ground pretty hard.

I drifted in the dirt toward the Durango. Then I got out of my car, leaving the door open and the engine running.

Shattered glass and pieces of the Durango lay everywhere. I could smell gasoline. Then I heard someone groaning and trying to push the front passenger door open. It was Davis! His head was covered in blood, and he spat blood out of his mouth. One eye was bruised and swollen, but he opened the other eye and saw me.

"Having a bad day aren't you?" he grunted.

"Where's Leah?" I yelled.

"I wouldn't tell you even if I could," he said, sneering. "You have no idea who you're dealing with or what you're doing. You . . . you're a lone sheep fighting wolves. You won't survive this."

The body of the dead man next to him was covered in a tactical vest, a couple of grenades hooked to it. I grabbed them.

"Yeah, you're probably right about that," I said as I pulled the safety pins off the grenades. I held one grenade in my left hand and the other in my right hand. "I'm a lone sheep, and I probably won't survive. But you know what?" I released both of the fuse pins on the grenades. "Neither will you." I tossed the grenades onto the Durango's undercarriage, and they landed next to the gas tank.

I walked toward my car. When I was halfway there, I heard Davis scream right before the grenades went off. The ground shook.

Sirens announced the impending arrival of emergency teams and backup cops. I jumped in my car and hightailed it out of there, terrified.

CHAPTER 18

My phone rang as I pulled into my driveway. I got out of my car and looked in all directions to see if anyone had followed me.

I didn't answer the phone right away. I wasn't sure what to say. I leaned up against the front fender of my car and eventually worked up the courage. When I answered, I assumed it was Alonso.

"She better not be hurt," I said.

"Josh?"

It was Leah!

"Leah! Oh my God! Are you alright?"

"Josh? Josh, I love you—"

"Enjoyed hearing her voice?" Alonso asked.

"Better than yours," I said.

"I've been seeing you on every news network. You've been a loose cannon, causing quite a scare in this city, breaking into the federal building, shooting up a dealership, killing cops at the gas station."

"They weren't real cops if they were on your payroll," I said. "Killing them was doing society a favor."

"You sound proud of what you did. So tell me, how much longer are you gonna keep this up?"

"I'm gonna do what it takes, no matter how many bullets I have to fire or how many of your men I kill. I'll turn the whole nation upside down if I have to."

Alonso chuckled. "I've never dealt with a guy who's as persistent as you. Usually, when I want someone dead, it happens with one bullet. But not you. For some reason you just won't disappear. You're like a . . . a wasp that keeps coming back to sting, no matter how many times you slap it."

I thought about the background on Alonso that I'd stolen from Frank's computer. One particular crime had made headlines across the nation.

"I remember, a long time ago, an incident happened in Los Angeles," I said. "I was really young at the time. I forget the guy's name, but he was . . . um . . . a neurosurgeon. Very wealthy man, respected in his community, well known. He had two daughters and a wife he'd been married to for thirty-five years. He lived a dream that everyone wished they had—success, independence, a beautiful family. But all of that was taken away from him one night when four men broke into his home, tied up his family, and looted the place. They beat the husband almost to death, putting him in a coma. Then they shot his wife, brutally raped, beat, and tortured those girls, then shot and killed them. The wife died later at the hospital. The man survived, barely. When he came out of his coma after several weeks, the police told him his family was dead. I can only imagine his heartache. Then, to make matters worse, justice was never served. No arrests were made. Neighbors told investigators they thought it was cartel related, so they never testified. Those men stole every bit of happiness from the man, and nobody had the courage to help him. They were afraid for their lives."

"I remember that story," Alonso said.

"Yeah. And here we are twenty years later, and I'm talking to the prick who destroyed that man's life. Small world, isn't it?"

"You think you know me?" Alonso said.

"I know exactly who you are and what I'm dealing with. You see, that surgeon and I have something in common. The newspaper stated he never knew who his parents were. He grew up in the foster system and didn't have any family until he met his wife and had children. Leah and her parents are the only family I've ever had. I'm a believer. I'm a Christian who believes in Jesus Christ as my Lord and Savior. Most Christians I know would tell me to sit and pray for the best in a situation, but I also believe in action. I made Leah a promise that I would always be there for her, to protect her. I'm not gonna break that promise."

"I'm pretty impressed with you," Alonso said. "You're not a coward. I respect a man who can fight when he feels it's necessary. Everyone else has run away. But you didn't. I respect that about you."

"I will find my girlfriend, Alonso. I'll also find you."

"How about we meet instead? I'll bring Leah with me."

"Where?"

"There's a parking garage on West Eighth Street right next to Interstate 110. Not a very busy place. Be there in a couple of hours when the sun goes down."

"I'll be there."

"Don't be late."

"Believe me, I won't."

I hung up. I knew Alonso would probably have twenty men with him. I needed a plan. Fast.

CHAPTER 19

The sky was clear and pitch black with a sliver of a moon and many stars.

I was standing on the top floor of a ten-level parking garage with my pistol in my pocket, surrounded by several vehicles. The rest of the building was packed. It was well lit near the light post, so I felt relatively safe, but it was eerily quiet. Way too quiet, except for the sounds of the city below.

After several minutes, I saw LED headlights from three vehicles coming toward me, two Ford Expeditions with a Ford Transit cargo van between them. Then another vehicle appeared—a black Jeep Wrangler Unlimited—and parked on the other side of the building. I didn't know who was driving the Jeep, but I was thinking it could be the observer. My heart began to race.

Four men holding assault rifles and submachine guns got out of each Expedition. I recognized Alonso and Juan. Alonso was wearing a tan suit and tie. Juan was in full tactical gear and holding a CZ Scorpion submachine gun. He had a Desert Eagle in his holster. Another four men got out of the Transit.

Alonso grinned at me.

"Joshua! It's so wonderful to finally meet." He looked me over.

"You're good looking. I can see why Leah loves you." Then he noticed the cuts on my face. "Whoa! What happened to your face? You get in a fight?"

"You could say that."

Alonso chuckled.

"Where is she?"

Alonso didn't answer me. Instead, he looked at Juan and nodded. Juan strapped his CZ Scorpion to his back, walked over to the Transit, and slid open the side door. He pulled out Leah, who was draped in a black sheet, her hands tied behind her back. He pushed her toward me. As they came closer, he removed the sheet. I nearly threw up. Leah's face was bloody and swollen. She had a black eye, and cheeks were bruised. Her nose and the corner of her mouth were bleeding. Her hair was matted with blood, and her clothes were dirty.

"Leah!" I cried in anguish. My heart broke.

"Josh!" Leah took two steps toward me. She was weak and trembling. Juan pulled her back, drew out his Desert Eagle, and pointed it at her cheek.

I pointed my pistol at him, and then all the other men surrounding Leah pointed their weapons at me.

I glared at Alonso. "I thought you said she wasn't hurt."

"She's alive, isn't she?" he replied. "I mean, a little banged up but alive."

I took two steps closer.

"Leah, babe," I said.

"That's close enough," Alonso said as he pointed his Springfield XDM pistol at me. I stopped in my tracks but kept my pistol pointed at Juan.

Alonso put his head up close to Leah's head and sniffed her neck. My stomach turned, and I felt a vein in my neck pulsing.

"She's pretty isn't she?" he said. "Hand me your gun."

"I don't think so," I said.

"I'm not asking."

I didn't give it up.

"You don't really think I came here just to chat, do you?"

"I'm not here just to shake your hand' that's for damn sure," I retorted. I bent my wrist slightly back to look at my smartwatch to see how much time I had. A minute and a half.

Juan pushed Leah over to another guy, then walked up to me and pointed his Desert Eagle right in my face. I returned the favor by pointing my pistol back at him.

"Hand it over, puta," he said, "or I'll kill you right in front of her."

I planned to make my move after the timer ran out. I handed my pistol to Juan with a smirk on my face, and waited with bated breath.

Juan grabbed the back of my hoodie and pulled me over to Alonso, face to face. Alonso put his XDM pistol back in his suit and came a little closer to me. Juan kept his tight grip on me.

"I underestimated you," Alonso said. "You have caused me more problems than I imagined. You slowed down my operation, and you killed a lot of my men. You're going around this city like you think you're playing Fortnite. I think you need to understand something. Your girlfriend's father put mine in prison. He destroyed my family."

"Your father got what he deserved, and now you're going to pay for what you've done."

Alonso punched me in my cheek, and I felt it bleed. Then he punched my stomach, sending me down on my hands and knees.

My watch showed thirty seconds left.

Juan pulled me back to my feet and held my hands behind my back. I counted down in my head as Alonso continued. "You know, at the beginning it was nothing personal. It was simply me doing business, asking Frank to go a different direction away from us, but he didn't. He decided to play hero and get in our way. Now it's personal."

I slowly lifted my head and glared at him. "After last night when you called me," I said, "it's been nothing but personal."

Alonso pulled out his pistol and pointed it at my face. "You made a mistake coming by yourself," he said. "But I'm not gonna kill you right here. I'm gonna take you with us, and I'm gonna torture you so bad that you'll beg to die."

Ten seconds left.

"That's where you're wrong," I said. "I didn't come alone. I brought three others with me."

Five seconds left, I thought. *Oh Lord, brace me for what's about to happen!*

"They all have one thing in common," I continued.

"And what would that be?" Alonso asked.

Three, two, one . . .

"Light." My watch beeped, and three pipe bombs I'd made at home with fertilizer exploded. The sky lit up, and the parking garage shook violently. I'd placed the bombs under vehicles at the edges of the garage. Cars went flying in the air like toys. A Chevy Tahoe went over the edge, to the street, and we were all knocked off our feet and sent flying too. Multiple car alarms sounded amid the flames and debris.

I saw everyone flat on the ground. Several men looked dead who were near by the bombs. *Thank God the debris didn't kill Leah,* I thought. She was flat on her stomach. She lifted her head and saw me.

I grabbed my pistol off the ground and ran to her.

"Leah, come on!" I yanked her to her feet, and we ran toward the staircase. "My car is at the bottom of the garage!"

A man behind us fired his machine gun, and the bullets shattered the glass in the staircase awning.

Leah screamed as we flew down the stairs to level nine. There, we had to sprint across to the staircase that went to level eight. Then we hid on level eight beside a parked SUV.

"Josh!" Leah threw her arms around my neck and sobbed. I put my arms around her back. "I knew you'd come for me," she said.

"Of course." I held her tightly and kissed the side of her head. She nudged her head into my shoulder. "Let me see your face real quick." When she did, I realized she was going to need stitches. I was furious. "Who did this to you?"

"The guy who hit you," she said, referring to Alonso.

She kissed me again. I really needed that. But we had to focus because Alonso's men were reaching our floor.

"Encuentralos!" ("Find them!") one of them yelled.

I grabbed Leah. "We need to get outta here. Come on!"

We ran for the other side of the garage to reach level seven.

Tires started screeching above us.

"Alli estan!" ("There they are!") I heard a guy behind us say, and then he began shooting.

"Get back!" I yelled, pulling Leah behind a Toyota Highlander. Two of Alonso's men were hiding behind us by a concrete support post.

"Josh, what do we do?" Leah whispered.

"We have to get to my car." I leaned over the Highlander's hood and fired two shots at the men but missed.

Then we saw the Jeep coming down the ramp from level nine. The driver saw us and stopped, and two guys got out.

A guy inside the Jeep pushed the rear hard top off, and I saw that the cargo area had two mini-guns mounted to the floor. The guy climbed onto the platform for the mini-guns. I was so scared I couldn't move.

"L-L-L-Leah?" I stuttered.

"What's wrong?"

"Leah, I th-think . . . I think we should . . ." Then the guy pointed the mini-guns at us. When Leah saw them, her eyes went wide.

"Run!" I screamed before the guy fired.

We hightailed it for the staircase as the guy fired both mini-guns at us. Bullets sprayed, hitting cars and causing them to explode.

"Son of a bitch!" I yelled.

Leah and I ran to the staircase as bullets tore up the concrete under our feet. We rolled down the staircase to level seven.

"Josh, are you OK?" Leah screamed as she crawled over to me.

"I'm fine! We gotta get outta here!" I grabbed her hand, and we ran for the staircase to level six.

The Jeep's tires screeched toward us again, coming down the ramp from level eight to seven. When the driver saw us from the other side of the garage, he stopped. Then the guy in the rear of the Jeep fired both mini-guns, sweeping them across the garage. I grabbed Leah, wrapped my arms around her, and pulled her down to the ground as bullets flew over our heads. Two parked cars exploded beside us as bullets pierced them.

I fired several shots at the Jeep as it moved among rows of cars. One bullet shattered the Jeep's taillight.

Leah was lying on the concrete, her hands over her head.

I slammed another magazine in my pistol. "Leah, are you hurt?"

"No I'm fine!" she said, lifting her head.

The Jeep was speeding toward us. The guy with the mini-guns was holding onto the Jeep's roll cage and standing on the running board. He was holding something small and circular. I couldn't tell what it was, but I didn't want to stick around to find out.

"Come on, Leah!" I pulled her up, and we ran to the staircase and jumped down the stairs. The Jeep flew past us, and I heard something bouncing down the staircase. A frag grenade! It fell to the bottom of the stairs and rolled under a Toyota Tundra crew cab parked right next to us!

"Leah!" I grabbed her hand. Seconds later, the grenade detonated, and the Tundra exploded into flames as it flipped onto its side. The shockwave threw us to the ground.

We heard the Jeep's tires squeal again, so we hid beside a Ford F-150.

"What are we gonna do?" Leah asked, her eyes searching mine.

I looked into the bed of the F-150, which was full of tools and equipment. I grabbed a flare stick and attached it to a small propane tank.

The Jeep drove up and down lanes of vehicles, looking for us.

"Stay here," I told Leah.

I carried the tank several feet away from us, where the Jeep would drive by. Then I pulled the tip off the flare, creating a flame.

I ran back to Leah, and we watched the Jeep speeding toward us. I pointed my pistol at the tank.

My heart pounded as the Jeep got closer. The second it got near the tank, I pulled the trigger. The tank exploded, igniting the passenger side of the Jeep, but the Jeep kept going!

"That should slow him down, I hope. Come on!" I grabbed Leah's hand, and we ran down to level five. We couldn't hear the Jeep anymore. We raced down levels four and three without hearing the Jeep. Then on level two, we heard the tires again.

"These people don't know when to quit!" I said.

We ran to the last stairwell. The guy in the Jeep fired both miniguns, hitting a Pontiac G8 next to us. It exploded, sending debris flying and a side mirror straight into the back of my leg. It hit me so hard that I fell down the stairs.

"Josh!" Leah screamed. I landed on my back on level one, dropping my pistol. My leg felt broken. "Josh!" Leah jumped down the stairs. "Are you OK?" She tried to pull me to my feet. "Josh, come on!"

"Ahh-ahh-ahh! Ouch!" I howled in pain. "I think my leg is broken!"

The Jeep reappeared.

"Josh, he's coming back!" Leah said. "Can you walk?"

"I don't know!"

I tried to get on my feet. Leah gave me both hands and pulled me up. I rested my arm across her shoulders and limped beside her on one foot.

We hid behind a Cadillac Escalade EXT.

"Got any plans, Josh? Please tell me you do!"

I didn't, but I looked around and saw a Ford F-450 utility truck with long cylinder helium tanks. There was a dolly in the truck too.

"Leah, come with me!"

I limped to the truck. We sat the dolly on the ground horizontally.

"We're gonna load this dolly up with six of these tanks! After we load up the dolly, grab another tank! I'll show you why after!"

After Leah and I loaded the dolly up with helium tanks, We pushed the dolly into place with the flat ends of the tanks facing the Jeep. Then we grabbed another helium tank from the F-450.

"I don't know what your plan is, but do you think it'll work?" Leah asked.

"If it doesn't, I don't know what will. Alright grab one end."

Leah and I grabbed both ends of the tank, and we lined it up with all six pressure valves on the tanks on the dolly, on which we were going to drop the tank.

"As soon as I tell you, drop the tank!" I said.

The Jeep turned toward us.

"Now!" I yelled. Leah and I let go of the heavy tank. It landed on all six valves, releasing the pressure, which threw Leah and I off our feet, and the tanks took off like missiles. They slammed into the driver's side of the Jeep, shoved the vehicle right off its wheels and into two parked SUVs. The ensuing explosion killed the guys inside.

Leah and I got back on our feet.

"Wow!" she said as she scanned the scene.

"I don't think he'll be a problem anymore," I said. "Come on."

We walked past the entrance of the garage and down the street toward my car, which was parked in an alleyway.

"Josh, you need to go to the hospital," Leah said. "You can barely walk."

"That can wait," I said. "Right now, let's get you to your parents' place. It's the only place where you'll be safe.

"I can see your car," she said in the dark.

But I wasn't paying attention as I stepped into a small pothole filled with water.

"Aah!" I yelled, the pain causing me to fall.

"Josh!"

"Damn it!"

"Josh, come on, get up. Hurry!"

We heard tires screeching. I knew it was one of Alonso's Ford Expeditions.

"Oh God, Josh, they're back!"

The driver of the Expedition turned into the alleyway and sped straight at us.

I got back on my feet.

"Josh, what do we do?"

I would have to shoot the driver before he made his move.

He hit the gas and bore down on us. I fired a shot but missed. My second shot hit the top of the windshield. My third bullet shattered a side mirror. Then I put a hole in the windshield.

"Damn it! come on!" I yelled. This time I took a couple seconds to aim. When the Expedition got closer, I fired at the driver, killing him and splattering his blood onto the windshield. But that didn't stop the Expedition. Instead, the engine revved even faster. His foot was on the gas pedal, all the way to the floorboards! The vehicle veered off and smashed into the rear of a parked Chevy Malibu. Then it went airborne, flying straight at Leah and me!

"Leah!" I screamed. I pulled her to the ground with me as the Expedition flew over us. It landed and barrel-rolled until it stopped on its top.

"Leah, are you OK?"

"Yeah I'm fine," she said. I got back on my feet and gave her my hand.

"Come on! Let's get out of—" Automatic gunshots came from behind me, and I felt a bullet hit my upper back and come out my shoulder. "Aaaah!"

"Josh!"

My blood splattered, and I fell to the ground. I saw Juan pointing his CZ Scorpion at me with four other men, including Alonso, beside him. Another Expedition and the Ford Transit were driving slowly right behind them as they walked toward us.

When I tried to point my pistol at Juan, he fired another burst at me. One of the bullets hit my pistol, knocking it out of my hands and destroying it. The impact almost broke my hand.

The men came up to us, pointing their weapons.

"Sostenla! Todavía la Necesitamos!" Alonso said. ("Hold it! We still need her!")

Two of them grabbed Leah and held her arms. She started kicking and screaming.

Alonso grinned at her.

"Grita todo lo que quieras. Solo espera a que veas lo que voy a hacerle a tu novio," Alonso taunted. ("Scream all you like. Just wait until you see what I'm gonna do to your boyfriend.")

"Mejor no le hagas daño!" ("You better not hurt him!") Leah cried. "Si le haces daño mal—" ("If you hurt him bad—")

"Callate!" Alonso yelled at Leah.

The other two guys restrained my arms and held me up. Alonso and Juan walked up to me, all tough. Their eyes looked soulless. I was losing so much blood that I started to feel dizzy and disoriented. Juan side-kicked me in my stomach with his steel-toe boot. I went down on my knees, the two men still holding my arms.

"Josh!" Leah screamed.

Alonso yelled at his men. One let go of Leah's arm, pulled out a Glock 19, and pointed it at Leah's face.

Alonso walked up to me, face to face, and sighed. "You know, I'm amazed at you," he said. "You never give up. Even after everything that's happened to you, you just don't give up. Just so you understand, I was never afraid of you."

"Rot in hell," I replied.

Alonso pulled out his pistol and pressed its barrel into my chest. "You see, the thing about hell is . . . I'd rather rot there than serve in heaven."

He pulled the trigger. The bullet pierced my chest and came out my back. Blood gushed all over my clothes, and I fell to the ground. Blood ran out of my mouth, everything went blurry, and I was losing consciousness.

"Josh? Josh! Nooooo! Leah screamed and fell to her knees, sobbing.

"Llevarla de vuelta a la camioneta," Alonso told his guys. ("Take her back to the truck.") They pulled Leah by her arms toward the Transit while she screamed and kicked.

Alonso looked down at me and grinned, shaking his head. He and Juan and the other men walked away. I passed out.

CHAPTER 20

slowly closed my eyes. I couldn't move or hear anyone. I couldn't feel anything except my blood around me.

After a while it seemed like I opened my eyes. I didn't know how long I'd been lying there, but everything looked different. A light surrounded me. I heard a man's deep, warm voice. I didn't know if it was God, Jesus, or who it was, but it was very relaxing. It sounded like the voice was speaking right into my ear, like someone telling me a secret.

"I love you, my child. Your pain is my pain. Your tears are my tears."

I woke up. I wanted to be with that voice, but I was still lying in the alley. I still felt the light, but I didn't see it anymore. Gradually, I realized the ground was still covered with my blood, and I was still injured, but the pain was no longer as bad. I couldn't explain it, but I was able to move. Perhaps I hadn't just suffered a delusion. It must have been God. It was like the Lord brought me back to life like he did with Lazarus.

I rolled around until I was able to get back on my feet. Using a dumpster to hold on to, I took a few deep breaths. Then I looked up at the sky, closed my eyes, and said a quiet prayer. I heard sirens coming toward me. I let go of the dumpster and limped toward my car. I climbed inside, started the engine, and hightailed it out of there.

I drove home to clean my wounds enough to get by until I could get to the hospital. I took a shower, then used rubbing alcohol on a microfiber cloth to clean my chest and back. I wrapped a bandage around my torso and changed into a clean T-shirt and jeans. I was still wearing Leah's bracelet, and no way was I going to take that off.

I had to figure out my next steps. I had no firearm and no way to fight back. All I knew was that I had to get to Leah's parents to fix things between us and give them an update.

CHAPTER 21

t was time to face the music, to face my fears. What could be worse than walking into a police station at that moment? Going to Frank and Karen's house.

I parked my car outside the security wall of the neighborhood and climbed a tree next to it. I disabled the laser tripwire alarm by using a magnetic mirror off my refrigerator and then jumped over the wall, landing in their backyard. I didn't know what I'd say to Leah's parents. I was really nervous, but I figured I'd find the words once their front door opened.

"Please, God, help me," I uttered under my breath as I walked up the steps to their door. "You know the circumstances." I took a deep breath, rang the doorbell, and waited. My heart was racing.

Seconds later, Frank opened the door.

"Josh?"

"Frank, Listen to me! I can explain everything!"

"You son of a bitch!" He grabbed me by my shirt, pulled me inside his house, and shoved me into the living room, causing me to roll over the coffee table, knocking off everything that was on it and onto the floor.

I got back on my feet and, shocked that Frank had shoved me

like that. I didn't think he had it in him. I was pissed but amazed at what he'd done.

"Frank! I can explain everything!" I pleaded.

"What the hell, Josh? What the hell did you do? And how did you get through security?"

"Your neighborhood security doesn't know I'm here. Let's keep it that way."

"Where the hell have you been?"

"I just got back from visiting hell for a day. Can't you tell?" I said as I pointed to the injuries on my face. "I even got to meet Satan's children."

"Josh?" Karen called from the top of the stairs. She ran down, sobbing, her hand over her mouth. "Oh my God, Josh, what happened?"

"I told you to let me handle this, and instead you went and destroyed half the city, killing cops?"

"I didn't kill any cops, Frank! Those guys weren't cops!"

"You're seriously trying to convince me that you didn't kill those cops at USC?"

"I didn't kill those cops, Frank! That one killed himself! I was trying to get him to tell me where Leah was, and he put a gun to his own head!"

"What? For God's sake. And what the hell were you doing at the car dealership?"

"The GM of that dealership was on Alonso's payroll!"

"What about the gas station?"

"Those cops pulled a gun on me while I was filling up my car! They were dirty cops, Frank. Real cops don't walk around carrying full auto Uzis! Look, I've been searching for Leah all day. I've been chased, beaten up, and shot at, and I lost a lot of blood earlier, so you'll have to be patient with me 'cause I can't think too straight . . . or see straight."

Frank sighed. "You never do!"

"Frank, these people aren't the street thugs you put in jail every day! This is the cartel! They aren't juveniles! They're trained professionals with full tactical gear and automatic weapons! This guy you put in prison has eyes inside every burrow and the whole city in his pocket! There's no hiding from these people! Oh, by the way, Detective Davis? He was on Alonso's payroll."

"Where is he?"

"He's dead. He tried to kill me at the gas station."

"I can't believe this," Karen said, going pale and nearly fainting.

"Neither can I," Frank said. "You also broke into my office, stealing my pistol!"

"I didn't break into your office," I said. "You left your door open. It's not breaking and entering if you leave the door wide open."

"I want to find out what damage you've done because you're all over the news," Frank said, turning on the TV. Fox News was talking about the explosion at the parking garage and all of the other destruction. My picture was posted as the suspect.

Frank put his hand over his eyes, shaking his head. "You're blowing up parking garages now?"

"I didn't do any of that." The news showed the damage from the pipe bombs as well as the Jeep that Leah and I destroyed. "OK I may have done that."

"I don't believe this!" Frank said. "Do you realize that every cop in Los Angeles is looking for you?"

"I got to see Leah!" I said.

"You saw Leah?" Karen and Frank asked at the same time, their eyes wide.

"At the garage," I said, nodding. "I tried to escape with her, but we got ambushed, and they took her again."

"Oh my God . . ." Karen started gulping for air and sobbing.

Just then someone pounded on the front door. Frank walked to the security monitor. "Oh my God! It's Agent Carter!"

I started panicking. Agent Carter was one of the FBI agents we'd met at the house.

I leaned around the corner of the wall and saw him and a group of men through the window in the door. This was bad.

"They're probably here for you!" Frank said.

"Frank, listen, they cannot—and I mean they *cannot*—find me here! If they do they'll arrest me, and you will never see Leah again! I have to hide!"

"Come on, Josh!" Karen grabbed me and hurried me up the stairs.

"Are you crazy?" Frank asked, glaring at her.

"I believe him!" she snapped. "You take care of those agents."

Karen put me in a hall closet.

"Don't make a sound," she whispered. Then she went downstairs.

In the dark I strained to hear the conversation.

"Hello, Agent Carter," Frank said, greeting them at the door.

"Mr. Rodriguez," Carter replied. "Mind if we come in? It's important."

"Come in," Frank said. I heard footsteps inside.

"Have you seen your daughter's boyfriend today?"

"No."

"Well . . . he's in a lot of trouble."

"Trouble? What did he do?"

"You haven't seen the news?"

"No, I've been trying to figure out how to save my daughter! Can you just cut to the chase?"

"He's wanted for murdering several of our officers. Have you seen or spoken to Josh at all today?"

"No, we haven't," Frank said.

"The last time we saw Josh was yesterday," Karen added, coming down the stairs.

"We have a warrant," Carter said. "Can we take a look around your home?"

I heard the agents begin searching for me. I knew I couldn't stay in the closet because they would find me if I did. I pushed the door open a crack, so I could see Leah's bedroom across the hallway. She had a balcony outside her room. I could jump and grab onto the gutter and climb up onto the roof. Then I could hide somewhere else.

I tiptoed into her room and closed the door. There were agents outside, so I had to be careful not to be seen as I slid the glass door to the balcony open and stepped outside.

As I turned around to close the sliding door, I saw an LED light from a flashlight coming under the bedroom door. It must have been an agent searching. I jumped, grabbed the gutter, climbed onto the roof, and walked to the chimney. I saw three agents walking around the backyard with their flashlights looking around the patio, the pool, and tennis court. I hid behind the chimney.

Moments later, I made my way to the roof of the garage, but then I had to jump over Karen's precious flower garden. I took a giant leap, landing on the edge of it and rolling onto the grass. A couple of seconds later, the sprinklers popped up and sprayed water all over the grass and into my face. I ran inside the garage before I was completely soaked. Then I heard the agents' voices.

"I'm gonna check the garage," one of them said.

My heart raced as I saw the door handle twist. I quickly lay beside Karen's Mercedes SL Roadster before the agent came inside the garage. An LED beam flashed around the garage, and I heard footsteps approaching me. I tried not to breathe, but I had to move. I tiptoed to Frank's Range Rover and leaned low on the passenger side. I saw the agent's feet walking along Karen's Mercedes.

Then he stopped walking, which made me nervous. I saw him bend down on his knees. He was about to look under the cars!

Luckily, the Range Rover had a running board. I grabbed onto the edge of the roof rack and stepped on the running board just as the agent shone his light beneath the SUV. Thank God he didn't see my feet.

I had one more vehicle to hide behind, which was Karen's Chevy Tahoe. After that it was just a matter of staying hidden until the agent left.

The agent's footsteps came closer and closer. I decided to tiptoe over to the Tahoe's passenger side. A few seconds later, I heard the agent talk into his two-way radio.

"The garage is clear," he said. "I'm gonna go check the backyard."

"Copy," Agent Carter replied.

I looked under the Tahoe and saw the agent walk toward the back door. Once he got halfway there, I made the stupidest mistake I could have made at that moment. As I leaned up, I hit my head on the side-view mirror, making a loud thump.

The agent's footsteps stopped, and he pointed his flashlight in my direction.

I put my hands over my mouth. *Oh my God, oh my God . . .* I didn't have any place to hide—except for one spot. But there was no easy access.

The agent came over to the Tahoe and looked on both sides. He got down on his knees and looked beneath, but he didn't see me. I kept absolutely still, didn't breathe, didn't move a muscle. A few seconds later, he got back on his feet and started back toward the door.

Thank the Lord he didn't see me. I was hiding inside the undercarriage. I had grabbed the top of the gas tank, pulled myself up, and laid above the driveshaft. The chassis rails had hidden my sides.

After I heard the agent close the door and walk outside, I rolled out from under the Tahoe.

"That was close," I sighed.

I hurried up a staircase that led back inside the house and entered the dimly lit hallway, where I could look down over the living room from a balcony.

I saw two agents come into the living room from the kitchen, shining their lights. I lay flat on the carpet under the railing to hide.

"The whole place seems clear," one said.

"Yeah, I didn't see anything," the other replied. "Let's check upstairs one more time, and I think we'll be good."

Oh great! I thought.

I got back on my feet and was about to hide in a bedroom when I saw the door handle to the garage turn. Someone was coming in!

Seriously? I groaned inwardly. *These guys are everywhere.* There was nowhere to go, except . . .

I put one foot on the railing, jumped over the balcony, and was out of sight. Two agents came in from the garage and met up with the two agents in the hallway.

I looked down on them from above. Frank and Karen's living room ceiling had wooden beams that extended toward the roof. Mid-jump, I had grabbed one of them and stayed up there like Spider-Man, my hands and legs wrapped around it. I wished I had the ability to shoot webs! I moved up the beam like a monkey to the tip of the ceiling and remained hidden there. It would be hard to get down.

A couple of minutes later, after they'd searched all the bedrooms, the agents walked downstairs and back into the living room—right under where I was hanging!

Then Agent Carter, Frank, and Karen walked into the room.

"The house is clear, sir," one agent said.

"OK," Carter replied, then turned to Leah's parents. "We're really sorry about this, Mr. and Mrs. Rodriguez. But if you see Josh at all, please call me."

Everyone went to the front door. I waited until I was certain the agents were gone. Eventually, I heard the door close, car engines start, and vehicles drive away.

I was so angry at the agents that I felt like I was going to explode. Frank and Karen walked into the living room.

"Where's Josh?" Frank asked.

"I left him in the closet, but he wasn't in it when I checked on him," Karen said. "Josh?"

"Josh? The men are gone," Frank called.

I let go of the beam and landed on the edge of their cherrywood coffee table, breaking it as I rolled onto the floor. They jumped back in shock, their mouths wide open.

"Ouch!" I winced, rubbing my backside as I stood up.

"Oh my God, Josh!" Karen said, as she and Frank came over.

"Are you OK?" Frank asked, helping me to my feet.

"Sorry," I said. "I was hoping I'd miss that table."

"Were you really up in the ceiling?" he asked, incredulous.

"I don't play around," I said. "I haven't played around all day, and I plan on keeping it that way. Now, as for Agent Carter, what the hell was that all about? I heard every word of your conversation with that dickhead before you let him in your house!"

"Josh, listen," Frank said. "I'm angry too—"

"Leah is being threatened, he won't help us, and he has the nerve to come into your house for a completely different reason, which doesn't involve Leah at all!"

"Josh—"

"He spent the whole day looking for me?" I said, cutting Frank off. "My girlfriend's life is on a ticking time bomb. and they're trying to find me? I oughta have his badge!"

"Josh—"

"If Leah dies, I will have his badge! FBI, LAPD, I'll have all of their badges! So much for 'Protect and serve!' More like 'Protect and serve themselves.' That's how screwed up our law enforcement is!"

Frank and Karen didn't say anything. They knew I was right.

"Yeah. Neither of you have anything to say now, do you? At least I got to see Leah, unlike them."

Frank sat down on his couch with his hands over his head. Karen stood beside me, rubbing my back.

"When you saw, Leah, how did she look?" Frank asked, peering up at me with a pained expression.

At first I wasn't sure how to respond. I mean, how could I tell a parent that their child had been beaten?

"They've been beating on her. Her face was bruised up pretty bad."

Karen broke into gulping sobs, her hands over her mouth.

"And when I talked to her on the phone, she wasn't too responsive," I said.

"Oh my God. My baby girl!" Frank broke down sobbing too. "All of this over one person I threw in prison."

I sat down on the loveseat, trying to think of a way through all this. It seemed impossible.

"It's like one of those bad dreams that people have once in a while, and they try to wake themselves out of it," I said. "I've been wondering if it's just a bad dream, but no, it's reality. In reality, you can't stop the bad dreams, but you can control what goes on in them. And that's why I'm not giving up on saving Leah. This is our bad dream, and I'm gonna take control of it until it ends."

"Josh, you can't go back out there and keep fighting these people," Frank said.

"I'm not stopping until I get to her," I replied. "I've done it once, and I'll do it again."

Frank stood up. "Josh, I'm saying you can't because you don't have the authority."

I stood up and looked straight into Frank's eyes. "Excuse me? They're promising to kill my girlfriend!" I said. "I've had the authority, Frank! You of all fathers should know what that feeling is like! I have one question for you, Frank. What progress have you made so far to help the situation?"

Frank didn't answer, just hung his head.

"Yeah. That's what I thought."

I walked away from him and began pacing.

He turned toward me. "What about *you*?" he snapped. "What progress have you made?"

"Well, for starters, I fought the people who kidnapped her!"

"Yes, but what progress have you made, Josh? Seriously, what have you done to help the situation?"

That was the million-dollar question, and I didn't have the answer. Other than fighting Alonso's men, I hadn't made any progress. And what was I going to do next? I had no idea. I felt stuck at a dead end.

"I . . . I don't know," I said. That was the only response I could come up with. "I don't know. I guess I'm out of moves. Look, the past five years I've had with Leah have been the best years in my life. She's the best thing I've ever had." I started tearing up. "She's family to me. She's the only family I've ever had . . ."

"Josh, Leah is not your family!" Frank said.

"Frank!" Karen said, glaring at him.

"Leah's your girlfriend," Frank clarified. "Girlfriend and family are two different things. Obviously that observation is lost on you—"

"Frank, that's enough!" Karen said. What Frank was saying really hurt me. Not only did it bring back memories about my parents abandoning me, after everything I'd done and gone through with Leah, I always thought she was family, and she always thought I was hers.

"Excuse me?" I said.

"Josh, don't listen to him!" Karen said

"Leah is my girlfriend of five years, and I love her!" I said. "She means the world to me!"

"You can't just say that Leah is your family because you don't have one of your own," Frank said. "I wish you would understand that!"

"Frank, stop it!" Karen said. "You're not helping anything here!"

"You're not a relative, Josh! You're just someone who my daughter brought home one day and who stayed around!"

I shook my head in anger. "How dare you?" I asked. "I stepped up when no one else would help you. I went after these people and took the law into my own hands. You got us into this situation, but you never went out there once to find Leah. You know what, Frank? You're right. I'm not a relative. But the thing about relatives is they are no more than blood. Family is about love . . . not that you would know what love is since you don't give your own daughter—or even your own wife—enough of it!"

"That's enough!" Karen said. "Both of you!"

"I honestly don't understand why Leah is still even with you after all these years!" Frank said. "I thought you would just be another one of her failed relationships!"

"You son of a—"Then I did something I'd been thinking might happen someday. I punched Frank in the face as hard as I could, and it knocked him down.

"Josh!" Karen screamed. "Oh my God!"

"What do you think of me now, Pop?" I said. "I'm more than just a punk with a crotch rocket—"

Frank shot back onto his feet and charged, slamming me into a glass display case, which then tipped onto the floor. Shattered glass flew everywhere.

"Frank! That's enough!" Karen screamed. She ran to him while he was on top of me. "Stop it!" She pulled him off me, and I got back on my feet.

"Josh, leave!" she yelled. "Now! Get out!"

"Alright, KAREN! Fine. I'll leave! But remember one thing, Karen, and one thing only." I pointed at myself. "I didn't demand action like Frank did! I took it!"

Frank's cheek was bleeding.

I stormed out of the house. I couldn't believe what had happened. I'd gone to Frank and Karen for help. Instead, I got into a fight. There was no rest for me anywhere. It seemed there was no hope either.

CHAPTER 22

The first thing I did when I got home was open a bottle of whiskey and drink and drink, shot after shot, because at this point I didn't want to be sober; I didn't want to feel anything honestly.

I sat on my front porch steps with my head resting against the railing, not moving a muscle as I stared into the distance, the bottle and glass next to me.

The alcohol didn't make me feel better. Only two things would make me feel better: having Leah next to me, safe and sound, or feeling the love of Jesus Christ.

I looked up, and to my surprise I saw Karen pull up in my driveway in her Mercedes. She walked toward me. I didn't even focus on her as she approached me. I just stared into the distance.

She sat down next to me, and neither of us said a word. After a while she waved her hand in front of my face to see if I was actually present in my body or if I was dead on the inside.

"What are you doing here, Karen?" I asked quietly.

"I've been trying to call you," she said. "You wouldn't answer, and I got worried."

"I didn't feel like talking," I said.

"I understand. You seem a little calmer now."

"Yeah, it's called whiskey."

"Well, if you don't mind, I'm going to have some with you because wine isn't cutting it for me." She took the bottle and poured herself a shot.

I continued staring into the distance. I didn't say a word.

"Josh, I have to ask you . . . why did you get involved the way you did today? You could've run away and been free from all of this."

I didn't know what to say. My head was full of thoughts. I took a deep breath and made an attempt to answer. "When someone does something unspeakable to someone you love, it . . . it messes with you. There are some things in life that you just can't walk away from because if you do, it'll haunt you till you take your last breath."

Upon hearing this, Karen quickly inhaled and let out a deep sigh.

"Josh, um . . . after you stormed out of the house . . . Frank and I talked and he wanted —."

"Why are you still married to him?" I turned to look her straight in the eyes.

"What do you mean?"

"You know exactly what I mean. Why do you put up with him, knowing you don't have to? Frank does nothing but put you and Leah down. He makes you and Leah feel like you're no more than investments. Does he even love you at all? You know I've never heard him say 'I love you' to you and Leah in the past five years I've been around your home. I've never even seen him hug you."

"Frank has never cheated on me, he's never lied—"

"You're right. He hasn't cheated or lied, but he does put his job before you. I remember one time Leah told me there had only been three people who had ever been there for her, and that was you, Karen, and me. Look, I'm sorry to come out this way about Frank, OK? But it hurts me when I'm forced to sit there and watch him verbally abusing you! And when he does, you just sit there and take it! I know damn well that I've never had a family. But I also know that a husband is not supposed to do that to his wife. You deserve better. I want better than that for you."

Karen wiped tears off her face and nodded. "I know he puts me down all the time, Josh. I just didn't know whether anyone else ever noticed."

"Karen, I've noticed since day one. And the way he treats me just proves it all. He even told me that he always thought I was just some punk kid that Leah picked up off the street."

Karen smiled.

"What?" I asked, surprised by her reaction.

"I'm sorry but the way you introduced yourself to him was classic. It wasn't exactly a smart way."

"There's a *right* way with him? I apologize. I guess I should've shown up at your doorstep wearing a suit and tie and driving a Rolls Royce."

"You know what I mean. You showed up in our driveway with a skateboard, no helmet, and you were dressed like a 1990s backstreet boy."

"I didn't have a car," I said.

"Frank wanted to shake your hand, but instead you fist bumped him and said, 'Yo, waz up, pop? Dude, nice crib. I bet you throw some dope legit parties up over here!'"

"I was twenty!" I said. "I'm more mature now."

"And let's not forget the time you and Leah threw a pool party while Frank and I were out of town."

"OK, OK. I get it. So I didn't make a good first impression. By the way, that pool party was Leah's idea. I was just the boyfriend who was dumb enough to go along with it."

We both laughed.

Karen took another shot of whiskey. "I remember how pissed Frank was when we came home, heard the loud music, and saw all of Leah's friends jumping around all over the house. Do you know where you were during the party?"

"I actually don't remember."

"Yeah, because you were passed out on the couch. Great first impression, Josh."

"Yeah, but that was before I became a Christian. I remember Frank blamed all that on me."

"Yes, he did." Karen smiled.

It felt good to laugh together. Pity that Frank still couldn't laugh about it.

"All of that aside, Josh, I've always liked you because you were good to me, and you were good to Leah."

"Well, I hope you like me . . . because, honestly, Karen, most of the time I feel like all Leah and I have is you. But hey, what do I know? Despite how long Leah and I have been together and how many times she's told me I'm part of your family, I'll never—"

"You need to ignore what Frank says and does to you," Karen said. "This is what's important: you have been so good to Leah. You love her, and she loves you. You've done so much for our family, through the good times and the hard times. You've given us nothing but love and support. And what you're doing right now for Leah is what family is all about."

"I once told Leah that I'd always be there for her. I'm a man of my word, and that's a promise that I'll take to my grave for her."

Karen grinned and put her hand on my back. "I always knew there was more to you than meets the eye," she said. "I was going to tell you that Frank and I had a long talk about things, and he wanted me to tell you that he came to a realization and wants to apologize to you about what happened earlier. He wants to come over here, but he's kind of afraid of you now."

"I'm really sorry about that," I said. "Is he OK?"

"He's just happy you didn't break his cheekbone. You hit him pretty hard. When I left the house, he was sitting on the couch with an ice pack over his cheek, moaning and groaning like he was going to die. Basically, the same way he does when he has a cold."

We both chuckled. I couldn't make fun of him though because I couldn't handle a cold either.

"He also wanted me to give these to you." She handed me a file packet of papers. On the front of the packet, Frank had written, "Please save my daughter."

"What's this?"

"Documents with information that Frank thought you could use. He found out that you took his other documents, but he printed these and thought you could use them instead."

I opened the packet and found info about Alonso's lawyer. *Perfect*, I thought. Here was the address to his office and details about what he knew about Alonso's operation. This was my golden ticket.

"Karen, this is exactly what I need! This is what will lead me to Leah! I can find her with this!"

"I know you will," Karen said with a grin. "Frank and I believe in you, Josh."

I closed the packet and beamed at her. "Thank you, Karen, so much," I said. "Tell Frank I said thank you also. I'm gonna do everything I can. I'm gonna get your daughter back. I'm gonna get my girl back, and everything will be OK."

Karen hugged me and kissed my cheek. "Go get her, gladiator," she said, smiling.

I smiled back at her. "Yes ma'am," I said. I kissed the palm of Karen's hand and then I made my way to my GTO.

"So what are you going to do next?" Karen asked.

I opened the driver's door and looked up at Karen. "Let me just say, I'm about to make a lot of noise."

With that, I took off down the road.

CHAPTER 23

Jacob Hudgens was an American lawyer who'd been on Alonso's payroll for decades and had spent a lot of time buying off judges and lawyers, according to Frank's notes—dirtier than words could say. But he wasn't going to be anyone's problem when I was through with him. One way or another, I'd make him talk.

I parked outside his office and was about to go inside, but something told me to wait in my car in the dark next to the parking garage to see who might pull in or out. After ten minutes I saw the LED headlights of an Audi R8 Spyder sports car. Hudgens drove it into the garage. A $250,000 car, bought with dirty money.

I followed him slowly down the ramp into the underground garage. It was almost empty, and nobody was around. Perfect, I thought.

Hudgens parked in a corner spot. I stopped my car in a lane and walked toward him as he sat in his car, looking at his phone. I opened the driver's door and punched him twice in the face. Then I grabbed him by the back of his head and smashed his face into the steering wheel, making the horn sound off. Then I slammed his head between the door and the door jamb, knocking him out instantly.

I duct-taped his hands and feet together, grabbed his arms, and pulled him out of the Audi and over into the trunk of my car. I slammed the trunk shut, adrenaline pulsing through my veins. Then I drove to my next destination.

I was just getting started.

Twenty minutes later in an abandoned warehouse, Hudgens was lying on his back on the concrete floor next to my car, out cold. I sat in the driver's seat, my door open and the parking brake on with the transmission in neutral. As he came to, he looked around, then looked at me. I grinned.

"Whoa!" he said. "Y-y-you . . . you're that kid!"

Hudgens tried to move his feet and hands but then realized I had restrained him. Then he realized what I was going to do next.

When he was knocked out, I wrapped a set of heavy-duty chains around his wrists and the other end of the chains around a concrete post. I had another set of chains wrapped around his waist and that set of chains circled around another post and then the end of the chains hooked to my car's rear axle. If Hudgens didn't talk, I was going to rip him in half. I had it all set up in a V pattern, so I could be next to Hudgens and watch him from my car.

"Quite a situation you got yourself in," I said.

"Let me go!" Hudgens said. "Let me go! Please, we can talk this out!"

"Oh we're gonna talk alright," I said. I got out of the car and walked up to him. "You see my car right there? That's a 2006 Pontiac GTO. Six-liter V8, 400 hp with 400 foot pounds of torque. That's a powerful engine for a car that size. Now, here's what's gonna happen. You're gonna tell me what I want to know, and I won't hurt you. If you don't, well, let's just say I wouldn't recommend that."

I walked back to my car, got inside, released the parking brake, and put it into first gear, but I held the clutch down to keep my car from moving forward.

I got my phone, pulled up a picture of Leah, and showed it to Jacob. "Where is she?"

"Go screw yourself kid!" he said. "You hear me? Go screw your—"

I let off the clutch, and my car moved forward, the chain pulling Hudgens up off the ground. "H-h-hey! Stop! Stop!"

I brought my car to a stop, put it in reverse, and backed up slightly to release some tension off him.

"You're gonna tell me what I want to know . . . or not," I said. "Where is she?"

"You have no idea what you got yourself involved in!" Sweat was pouring down his forehead.

"Wrong answer," I said as I moved the car forward again, this time even farther.

"Hey-hey-hey! Stop!" Hudgens screamed. "Stop! Let's talk!"

I stopped my car right there. "Let's try that again," I said. "Where's my girlfriend?"

He didn't answer. I revved my engine, making the loud exhaust rumble.

"Son of a bitch! I'm a lawyer! Do you have any idea what I can do to you?"

"I don't have a lot of time, which means you don't have any. Look at me, old man! It's a simple question. I'm giving you the option to keep your life. All I want to know is where your men are keeping her."

No response, so I moved my car forward again, stretching Hudgens even more.

"Aaaaah! Aaaaah! Stop!"

I stopped my car completely. "OK," he sputtered. "OK, listen to me! I know where your girlfriend is, but you won't be able to get inside of where she is."

"Where?" I asked.

"There's a warehouse over at Terminal Island. That's where he does his operation. Nobody can get inside. It's secured."

"I want to get in."

"Kid that's easier said than done. I can tell you this: you won't be able to get inside with weapons that you see at your local gun shop. You're gonna need military-grade weapons. Alonso has an oil complex. There's a bunker under the complex with an armory room full of military weapons. Anything you can think of, he's got it. You won't be able to enter it by yourself. But I can. Let me go, and I can take you there, alright? Please!"

It sounded like he was telling the truth. He was scared enough. I put the gearshift in neutral, pulled the parking brake, then got out of the car and walked over to Hudgens.

"Look at me," I said. Hudgens looked up into my eyes, scared. "I'm gonna take you to that bunker, you're gonna get inside, and you're gonna get me everything I need, or I'm gonna hurt you very badly."

I unhooked the chains, threw him back in the trunk, and made my way over to Alonso's warehouse.

CHAPTER 24

ifteen minutes later, I parked my GTO in the far back of the parking lot outside the oil complex. I grabbed Hudgens out of the trunk and cut the tape off his legs and feet.

"Move it," I said, keeping him in front of me as we walked toward an area that looked like a military complex. Semi-trucks with tanker trailers were pulling in and out. Thousands of oil pipes ran all over the place from a massive storage building in the center.

"You guys seriously have an armory bunker under an oil complex?"

"Let me put it this way," Hudgens said. "When you have the money Alonso has, you can have whatever you want, wherever you want."

"You'll need access to get through the entrance," he said. "You'll have to stay right beside me if you want to get in."

"All you have to do is get me to that armory room, and you'll be free to go," I said.

The door slid open as we walked into the entrance, and then we came to a door that required a keycard. Hudgens reached for his wallet, got his card, and slid it into the reader. The door opened, and we walked into an eerily empty lobby.

We came to an elevator where Jacob slid his keycard in again. The doors opened, and we walked inside. We went down for a while, and the doors slid open. Ahead of us was a hallway. We walked toward the bunker.

Everything looked state of the art.

This is crazy, I said to myself, studying the complex. "I can tell my tax dollars treat you guys well," I muttered to Hudgens. He glared at me. At the end of the hallway was a large armored door. It slid open as we approached. Hudgens had told the truth.

God Almighty, I'd never seen so many military-grade weapons, machine guns, full-auto assault rifles, grenades, rocket launchers . . . everything was full-on tactical. Alonso had enough in the room to start a small war, which was what I was about to do with him.

"Oh my God!" I said in amazement.

"These are the weapons you'll need," Hudgens said. "Anything you need is in here."

"I think I've got more than I expected," I said. I grabbed a G36C SBR machine gun with a red-dot scope and a flashlight attached to the rail system. "This is unreal." I grabbed a magazine, loaded it, and cocked the machine gun. "Wow."

Hudgens pointed to the other side of the room. "Tactical vests, ammunition, and grenades are over there."

I turned my back on him. A few seconds later, I heard a click. I pivoted and saw him pointing his Glock 42 at my face. He pulled the trigger, but the Glock only clicked.

"Missing something?" I reached into my pocket and pulled out the firing pin that I'd taken out of his Glock. Back at the parking garage, I'd found that he had the weapon concealed under his pant leg. Instead of taking the bullets out, I removed the firing pin, so he wouldn't know the difference when he held it in his hand.

I dropped the firing pin on the ground and hit Hudgens in the face with the stock of the G36C, knocking him to the floor. Then I stomped my foot on his chest and pointed the weapon in his face.

"Here's what I'm gonna do. I'm gonna kill you right here, and then I'm moving on—"

"N-no stop! Stop! Please listen!"

"Why should I?" I yelled. "You got me this far! Why try to kill me now?" He started tearing up and blubbering.

"You'd better start making your peace with God," I said, "'cause I'm gonna blow your head off!"

"Stop! Listen to me! This is not how my life was supposed to be. I never wanted to work for these people, OK?"

"What are you talking about?"

"My life changed!" He started talking faster than normal. "That's what happened! In the beginning I never wanted to do anything for these people. Back when I was in law school, I was on a tight budget, and I had a family to feed. I almost couldn't afford to continue classes. That was when I came across the Alonso family. They offered me a job, paid for my college, my home, took care of my family. They did everything as long as I worked for them."

I kept the G36C pointed at his face, but I took my finger off the trigger. He sounded like he was being honest.

I took the G36C out of his face. "Get up!"

He looked scared as he stood up in front of me.

"I'm gonna tell you something, and I want you to listen real good," I said. "You're lucky because two things are keeping me from killing you right now: my love for my girlfriend and my love of God. I believe in God, and I believe Jesus Christ is my Lord and Savior. I'm not trying to preach to you, but I understand the importance of forgiveness. If you think about it, Jesus and forgiveness go hand and hand. After Judas betrayed Jesus, Jesus was still willing to forgive him. After those Roman soldiers had beaten and tortured

Him for days before nailing him to the cross, Jesus was still willing to forgive them too. If Jesus could forgive those Roman soldiers after everything they'd done to him, I know I can forgive you—and that's what I'm gonna do."

He stared at me, shocked.

I set the G36C down on the glass table beside me. Sitting on the table was an armored crate with brick-sized blocks of C-4 explosives. I grabbed one.

"You realize you helped me, right?" I said. "Which means Alonso's gonna kill you. If I die tonight, you'll be dead tomorrow. If I don't, you're a free man. I'll leave this with you: I would leave LA for good, and take your family too. And I mean for good, for your safety. Go somewhere else: San Francisco, San Diego, out of state, I don't care. I wouldn't stay here anymore. Go start a new life, an honest life. Now go, and you may wanna hightail it."

"Why?"

I put my finger on the C-4 activation switch and flipped it. It made a beep. "'Cause I'm gonna blow the whole complex off the map," I said, and then I stuck the C-4 charge on a support beam.

Hudgens ran for the exit. I wondered if I'd made the right decision. Did I trust him? Absolutely not. It didn't matter though because once Alonso knew he'd led me there, he would kill him.

I pulled a black military-style tactical vest down from the wall and put it on. It had pouches on the chest and leg attachments with pistol holsters. I covered my knees and elbows with pads and donned tactical gloves and steel-toe shoes. In the holsters I put two Glock 17s, so I could pull them out and fire both at once. They both had compensators, giving them the Tomb Raider look.

I grabbed two fully automatic Glock 18s with red laser sights and thirty-three-round extended magazines and put them in my belt holsters.

I needed a shotgun. I found a double-barrel DP12 with a green laser sight and a flashlight. It had a sling with 12-gauge slug shells and dragon's breath shells, which would shoot flames out of the barrels like a dragon blowing fire.

I would need to approach Alonso and his men quietly at first, so I chose an HK433 full-auto assault rifle, chambered in 300 AAC blackout, which had a threaded barrel, so I could put a suppressor on it. It had a front battle grip with a flashlight and a blue laser sight built inside of it with a red-dot scope. Before heading out, I put several throwing knives in one of my pouches. I added some frag grenades, flash-bang grenades, and smoke grenades to my vest as well as pistol and rifle magazines. One last thought: multi-tool pliers. I also couldn't resist some tinted safety glasses. I figured I might as well look cool while protecting my eyes.

I was ready for battle, and I would use Alonso's own firepower against him. I began to rig up the bunker with C-4 and activate all of the charges. Once they detonated, the oil lines in the hallways that ran around the complex would explode, and the fire would destroy the building. On each support beam, I placed an activated C-4 charge. Then I grabbed the remote detonator.

"Time to get out of here," I said to myself.

I walked briskly down the hallway toward the elevator but something caught my eye. A door was open. It led to a huge room that was about the size of a basketball court. I could hardly believe my eyes. Several giant crates were filled with paper money. I stepped inside the room, carefully looking around me. Each crate was labeled, "One billion dollars."

I got a dark, creepy feeling from being around that money. It wasn't the money that bothered me; it was the history behind it. I knew it represented lives destroyed, families torn apart, people killed, drug trafficking, prostitution, businesses robbed . . .

"All of the lives you've ruined, all of the families you've destroyed, all of the crimes you've committed . . . just for what's in this room." I started tearing up and struggling to breathe. I reached for my DP12 from the back of my vest and started loading it up with dragon's breath shells.

I took a deep breath and wiped my eyes.

"The clock is ticking for you. I'm coming for you and all of your little bitch boys, and when I come down there . . . I'm gonna kill all of you."

I pumped my DP12, pointed it at the closest crate, and fired two dragon's breath shells. The crate instantly caught fire, and the flames spread quickly to the others around it. Just to make sure, I walked around them, pumping more shells into other crates until every crate was on fire. A river of sweat was streaming off me.

By then the entire room was ablaze.

CHAPTER 25

couldn't believe I was about to do this. All of Los Angeles was about to get an unexpected middle-of-the-night wake-up call . . . with a boom.

I walked through the parking lot toward my car. It was almost completely quiet outside except for cargo ships blaring their horns in the distance as they entered the harbor.

I grabbed the detonator and put my thumb on the button, preparing for the ground-rumbling explosion. I was shaking, but I had to be brave. I thought of all the people the cartel had harmed or could harm if I didn't. Then, after a few seconds . . . I pushed the button.

A loud boom shook the ground behind me, followed by aftershocks until the pipelines exploded into a huge ball of black-and-orange flames. The parking area lit up like it was daytime.

I pulled my Glock 17s from my holsters, loaded them with magazines, pushed both pistol grips together, and released the slides, putting a bullet in each chamber. I put the weapons back in my holsters, then grabbed my shotgun and loaded it with slugs. As I walked away from the flames, I felt like an action hero.

The oily fumes spread quickly as I hurried to my car and drove away from the complex, looking back in my rear-view mirror at what used to be an oil storage complex with a cartel bunker. Now it looked like hell had risen up. But we had squashed it. Me and God.

CHAPTER 26

I was speeding southbound on Interstate 710, overtaking car after car, doing over 100 mph. With my windows down and the sunroof open, the wind felt good on my face and arms after the dripping sweat from the burning fire back at the oil complex.

My phone rang. I looked at the touchscreen in my GTO and saw an unknown number. I answered it anyway because maybe it was someone I knew.

"Hello?"

"Is this Josh Daniels?" a man asked. I didn't recognize the voice.

"Who is this?" I replied.

"Agent Carter . . . FBI."

"Sorry, Josh isn't in," I said. "He's busy doing someone else's job. Can I take a message?" I was so angry at this guy, but probably being a smart mouth wasn't a good choice.

"Josh, we need to talk."

"I've got nothing to say to you."

"You will after I tell you why I'm trying to find you."

"You really think, after the day I've had, that I wanna talk to *you* guys? *You* have some explaining to do to *me*. Why is it that I've been doing all the dirty work trying to save my girlfriend? Her parents and I came to you guys for help, and you turned your backs on us.

"Josh, I know you're angry with us, but you have to hear me out. I know you've been looking for Leah, and I know about everything that's happened today. That's why you're on every news network."

"I guess I have you to thank for giving me my fifteen minutes of fame."

"Josh, hear me—"

"No! You know what? Screw you, cop! I'm done! After everything that's happened, I don't trust any of you!"

"Josh—"

"I don't care what you do!"

"Josh—"

"I don't care what you say about me, I'm not gonna—"

"Josh, I know you're innocent!" Agent Carter said.

That shut me up instantly. I wanted to hear exactly what he had to say. The only problem was, I wasn't sure if I wanted to believe him.

"I know you've been innocent this whole time. Listen to me, and please don't interrupt, OK?"

"I'm listening."

"I looked at the surveillance videos, we talked to eyewitnesses, and we looked into those cops' body cameras, which recorded everything they'd been doing since last week. Those showed us the men were dirty cops. The recordings also showed what happened at USC and the gas station. We know the cops were on Alonso's payroll. That takes you off the hook. So you don't need to run anymore."

"I've already had several of your guys in uniform try to kill me today, so give me one reason why I should trust you."

"Because I know where Leah is," he said. "When we arrested a few of our own guys, they confessed, and we confirmed that Leah's being held at a warehouse on Terminal Island. Listen, I know you don't trust us, but I'm not one of the bad guys, and neither are you. I was wrong about you. Everything I thought about you was wrong, and I'm sorry, buddy. Now, wherever you are, turn around and come over to Frank and Karen's house, so we can talk this out, OK?"

"I accept your apology, and I'm glad you know the truth about me, but I can't do that. You see, I've been investigating too, and I know Leah's at the warehouse. I'm going over there to save her."

"Josh, you can't! Listen—"

"No, you listen to me! I don't mean any disrespect to you, but I am not gonna rely on someone else to save my girlfriend. I made her a promise that no matter what, I'd always be there for her, and that's what I'm gonna do. I am going to that warehouse, and I'm getting Leah back safe and sound, and I'm going with or without you."

"So, there's no stopping you? Well, I guess I'll see you over there. Be careful."

"You too." I hung up. "Here I come, Babe," I whispered as I shifted into the highest gear and flew down the interstate, straight for the warehouse.

CHAPTER 27

The warehouse on Terminal Island was massive and heavily guarded by Alonso's men with state-of-the-art surveillance. I was about to sneak into a building guarded by the cartel. My head was screaming, and I was so stressed that I was sweating through my jeans and tactical vest.

I parked on a dirt road and then walked along the fence. On the other side was a train yard filled with train cars. The warehouse was just beyond that.

I planned to sneak through the railyard, but I couldn't find a gate or any other way through the fence. I couldn't climb it because it had razor-sharp wire on top, like the ones at a prison yard. So, I grabbed a pair of cutters from my tool pouch on my vest and began cutting wires until I could crawl through. There was no motion in the yard, so I darted between train cars and tracks until I made it to the other side.

I loaded my HK433, put a suppressor on the barrel, and turned on the blue laser sight.

"Alright, let's do this," I said, as I put on my safety glasses. I walked quietly along the warehouse until I saw an open door. As I drew closer, I heard voices inside.

I ducked behind a dumpster. When I peeked around it, I saw two guys walking in orange safety vests, holding assault rifles. When they passed me, I fired a burst of bullets into their backs, and the men fell to the ground.

No one else came out, but I still had to be careful because I was outnumbered until Agent Carter and his guys arrived. I walked through the door into a long hallway with rooms on both sides. All the doors were open, and I intended to check every single one.

I pointed my HK433 in front of me, turned on the flashlight in the front grip, and began walking down the hall, passing empty locker rooms and break rooms.

The next room had a square of glass on the door. Through it I could see TV and computer monitors and two guys wearing safety vests sitting with their machine guns on their desks. I hid behind the door.

There was a problem though: even though I had a suppressor on my HK433, it was still loud and would be even louder indoors. So, I decided to take out one of the guys with a throwing knife, then make the other guy tell me exactly where Leah was.

I strapped my HK433 to the back of my vest, grabbed a knife, and took a deep breath. I stepped forward and threw my knife as hard as I could at one of the men. It stabbed him in the back of the neck, and he fell off his chair. Blood began to pool on the floor. The other guy ran over to him and reached for his machine gun. I restrained the man's arm with one hand and grabbed the back of his neck with my other hand. Then I slammed his head into the desk and held his head against it.

"Where is she?" I asked. He didn't say anything. I pulled out a Glock 17 and pointed it at his mouth. "I will put a hole through your mouth if you don't talk!"

"Wait! Wait! OK! OK!" The guy said. "Monitor five! That's her on the screen! Section seven, room twelve on the third floor."

I looked at the monitor and saw Leah lying sideways on the floor in the corner of a room with concrete walls and no window. Seeing that made me even angrier. I held my Glock by the slide and hit the guy in the side of his head with the grip. It knocked him out instantly.

"Well, that wasn't hard." I said.

Ten minutes later I came to a door on the third floor and slowly opened it. It led to a balcony with a view of the shipping dock inside the warehouse. A cargo ship was moored inside the warehouse, and a crane was unloading containers from it. Then front-end loaders were moving them within the building. I had a feeling those containers held contraband.

I saw another door on the other side of the warehouse. I would have to crawl over to it because armed men were on the ground floor. Alonso and Juan were walking together. Both were in tactical vests and carrying several weapons.

I crawled along the balcony and found a door with a small square of glass in it. I got back on my feet, looked through the glass, and saw a large hallway with wooden crates stacked along the sides. The rooms on either side were numbered from one to twelve. Leah had to be in the last one!

I opened the door and walked to Room 12. Peeking through the window in the door, I was so relieved to see Leah, even though she was lying on the floor, her hands tied behind her back. I couldn't tell if she was awake or not, but I could see her breathing.

I tried to turn the doorknob, but it was locked and I didn't want to make any noise.

Then I heard a voice down the hallway.

"Vamos a sacar a esta perra." ("Let's get this bitch out.") Footsteps were coming toward me.

I panicked and hid behind a stack of wooden crates.

As the footsteps got closer, I peeked out and saw three men approaching Leah's door. One started unlocking it.

"Wakey, wakey, guisante dulce," (sweet pea) one of them said in a sarcastic tone, and the other guys laughed. They strode into the room and walked Leah out, with one guy restraining her by her arm. They went down the staircase to the bottom floor. *Most likely to Alonso*, I thought.

"Not my baby. No you don't," I whispered.

I went back to the balcony, so I could get a bird's eye view of what was about to unfold.

I saw the three men take Leah face to face with Alonso.

"Desatarla," ("Untie her") Alonso said, and one of the men cut her free. "It looks like I'm gonna have to cut your time short, sweetheart. After I do, your boyfriend and your mama and papa will be next."

One of the men was standing too close to Leah. She grabbed a knife out of his holster and slashed Alonso's face!

"Aaaaah!" Alonso howled as he put his hands on his bleeding face.

Leah charged at him, trying to grab one of his weapons, but two men grabbed her and slammed her onto the concrete.

Alonso was cursing, his face was covered in blood.

"Time to go loud and hot," I whispered as I took the suppressor off the HK433.

"Matar a la perra!" Alonso screamed. ("Kill the bitch!")

Leah started screaming and crying as a man pointed his shotgun at her face.

I pointed my HK433 at the guy's head. Once I saw the blue laser sighting on his face, I pulled the trigger. With an ear-splitting sound, the bullet pierced his brain, killing him instantly.

Blood splattered out both sides of his head, and his body fell to the floor.

Quickly, I shot and killed the other two men.

Alonso's other men took cover behind anything they could find. Alonso and Juan ran for cover elsewhere.

Leah looked up at the balcony and saw me.

"Josh?" she said, smiling.

"Hey, beautiful," I said. "I'm here for ya—"

A volley of bullets flew at me from automatic machine guns below. I hit the deck.

"Come on out, puta!" one of the men yelled.

"Yeah, sure!" I said as I lifted my HK433 over the balcony with one hand and blind-fired at some men hiding behind a shipping container. Then I jumped over the balcony railing, landed on a shipping container, and then jumped off and hid behind the corner of it.

"El esta escondido allí!" ("He's hiding there!") one of the men yelled as more bullets flew at me.

I fired at the group until my rifle was empty. Then I hid behind the container and pulled the magazine out of the HK433.

Damn, this thing is loud!

I put another magazine in, cocked it hot, leaned around the edge of the container, and fired, killing two guys.

Leah was in sight, lying on her stomach, her hands over her head as bullets flew over her. I had to get to her and quickly.

"Leah, I'm coming!" I yelled and then fired again at the men.

I wasn't going to be able to take out all those guys in plain sight, but I could if they couldn't see me. If I threw a flashbang and then a smoke grenade after that, I could come out and take out the men, one after another, while running for Leah.

"Leah! Cover your eyes!" I yelled.

I grabbed a flashbang and a smoke grenade from my vest, pulled the pin on the flash grenade, and threw it where every guy would see it. I covered my eyes. The grenade exploded with a loud bang and a bright flash that made the night look like intense sunlight.

Then I pulled the pin off the smoke grenade and threw it. About ten seconds later, the area was filled with white smoke.

Now was my chance.

I strapped my HK433 to the back of my vest, pulled out my Glock 18s, and turned on both red laser sights. Then I donned my blue-tinted safety glasses and charged into the smoke. The laser sights created a red beam, making it easier to aim.

All the guys were wiping their watery eyes. As I ran past them, I fired, killing them.

Leah was about twenty feet away from me, and I was running as fast as I could. But once I got close to her, I saw two guys come out from behind a shipping container. They didn't point their assault rifles at me; they pointed them at her.

"Leah!" I yelled. I dove while pointing my Glock 18s at the guys and fired both of them, killing our attackers. I landed on top of Leah, shielding her.

"Get up! Come on!" I yelled.

We ran for cover as someone behind us opened fire, barely missing us. Leah screamed.

"Leah! Keep going! Keep going!" I yelled, as I turned around, running backwards and pointing both Glock 18s at the guys shooting at us. I fired until both Glock's ran out of bullets

We jumped over a wooden crate, came to a shipping container, and hid behind it.

"Josh!" Leah said as she threw her arms around my neck, crying. "I thought you were dead!"

"I thought I was too," I said as I kissed the side of her head. I put my arms around her and held her as she sobbed.

Then I reloaded my weapons.

Leah stared, blown away at my vest and all the weaponry.

"Wha . . . Where did you get all this stuff?"

"You wouldn't believe me if I told you," I said as I released the slides on both pistols.

Looking over her shoulder, I saw four guys with assault rifles appear from behind a shipping container, weapons at the ready.

"I don't even care about that," she said. "I'm just so happy to see you."

"That's great, babe. I'm happy to see you too. Can you get down for a second?"

Leah ducked, and I fired both Glock 18s, killing all four of those guys. Leah screamed. Then she got back on her feet and looked at me.

"Are you OK?" I asked.

Just then I saw two more guys appear from behind another container with assault rifles aimed at us.

"Yeah, I think so—"

"I'm sorry. One more," I said. As Leah ducked, I pointed the Glocks at one of the guys, fired, and killed him. But when I tried to shoot the other guy, both Glocks clicked. They were empty!

I dropped one of my Glocks and grabbed a throwing knife out from my vest, then threw it at the guy. It landed in the center of his forehead, killing him instantly.

Leah got back on her feet, turned around, and saw the guys I'd just killed. She turned and faced me, shocked. I couldn't believe it either.

I reloaded my weapons and put them in my holsters. Then I grabbed my HK433. "Come on," I said. "We can't stay here."

"OK, John Wick, sounds good," she said weakly.

Bullets hit a container beside us. A couple of guys on the balcony above were firing their machine guns at us. I grabbed Leah by her arm and pulled her with me. We ran, dodging the fire, and hid behind a dumpster. The bullets bounced off the thick steel while we leaned against it.

While they were shooting at us, I heard Alonso's men laughing.

I held my HK433 on the corner of the dumpster and blind-fired a burst of bullets.

"You won't think it's so funny when I put a bullet in your head!" I yelled.

"Mata al chico blanco!" a guy on the balcony yelled, and then they resumed firing.

"Leah, what did he say? I didn't understand them."

"They said, 'Kill the white boy!'"

"Oh, really?" I strapped my HK433 back on my back and grabbed my DP12, since I was a little angry. I leaned over the edge of the dumpster, pointed my DP12 at one of the men, and fired one slug into his chest, killing him instantly. Then I took out the other guy with another slug.

I pumped the two shells out of my DP12.

"How do you like this white boy now, bitch?" I yelled to the dead guys I had just shot.

Another stream of bullets hit the dumpster, and I quickly hid behind it.

"Damn! These guys are everywhere!" The problem was, this time, I didn't know where the shots were coming from. They seemed to be coming from all directions.

Then I heard a helicopter.

"Josh, look!" Leah pointed up at the ceiling. Through the sky-light, I saw a spotlight moving around. "Is that the police?"

"I really hope so!" I said as more bullets hit the dumpster. "We have to get outside!"

"How?"

I saw an open drive-thru on the other side of the warehouse, but it was too far for us to reach without being shot, so I had to be creative again. Next to us was a flatbed pushcart. If I threw a flashbang grenade to blind the guys shooting at us and a smoke grenade to hide the area, Leah and I could lie on the flatbed and wheel over to the door. Meanwhile, I'd be firing at those guys. With the floor sloping down slightly, the cart would roll down faster than we could run.

"Leah, remember when we went skiing in Utah?"

"Yeah?"

"Remember how we sledded down the mountain?"

"What are you thinking?"

I grabbed the cart and grinned. It took her a second to figure it out.

"You can't be serious."

I pulled the push handle off, so the cart was completely flat. Then, I grabbed the grenades, pulled the pins and threw the grenades out into the open. They exploded with a searing flash of light, and then a thick cloud obscured our path to freedom.

I put Leah on her back on the cart. I strapped my DP12 to the back of my vest, grabbed my Glock 18s, and lay on top of her to shield her.

She wrapped her arms around me, closed her eyes.

"You ready?" I asked. She nodded. "Let's go!" I pushed off with both feet, and we rolled straight toward the blinded bad guys. I used the red laser sights on my Glock 18s, so I didn't have to aim. Rolling past a stack of wooden crates through the smoke, I saw three men hiding. I fired both pistols at the same time, killing all three of them.

We were rolling faster and faster down the incline, like we were in an ice race. Leah was clinging onto me for dear life, and I could barely breathe.

I saw two guys standing in the open, wiping their eyes. One saw us and fired his machine gun, but every shot missed us. I fired my Glock 18s and killed both of them, as we rolled past.

More guys came from behind the containers and crates, shooting machine guns at us. One threw a frag grenade. It landed on the floor as we rolled past. It exploded and shook the ground so badly we almost rolled off the cart. Pieces of concrete and debris flew everywhere.

The overhead door we were rolling toward started to close! *Oh, my God!*

"Leah, lie as flat as you can!" I yelled. She did, but I couldn't lie any flatter.

Our escape route was closing!

When we got to the door, it scraped the back of my vest as we narrowly ripped out into fresh air.

Unable to stop the cart, we smashed into a huge shipping container. I flew off one side of the cart, and Leah flew off the other.

I looked to see if she was mad at me for my crazy idea. Instead, she grinned at me as she got herself together.

"That was . . . fun," she said.

"You wanna go again?" I asked.

"No, I'm good."

We laughed.

"I didn't think so," I said. We got back on our feet, brushed ourselves off, and I reloaded my Glocks. I put them in my holsters and grabbed my HK433.

The sound of that helicopter got louder and louder until it appeared to be behind the warehouse. Eventually, we saw a black

Eurocopter AS350 with three guys inside, shining a spotlight on us. A guy in the back was holding an M249 SAW machine gun and another had a semi-automatic grenade launcher. Three news helicopters also arrived, making wide circles above the building.

The chopper descended, and we looked up at it, hoping to God these were the good guys.

"Josh Daniels!" a voice boomed. "This is the FBI. We've got the perimeter secured. Head for safety, and we'll cover you."

I was so relieved to see good guys for once.

"About time. I didn't think they actually cared," I said. I took Leah's hand, and we raced to the other side of the warehouse, where I'd first entered. The helicopter hovered beside us as we ran, the gunner keeping guard. It was surreal, like an action movie.

Then I saw two red Polaris RZRs speeding toward us! They stopped in front of us, and eight of Alonso's men got out, each with an assault rifle.

"Take cover!" the FBI ordered.

We hid behind a stack of fifty-gallon oil drums.

The chopper flew toward the men. The gunner with the M249 opened fire, killing five of them. The other gunner fired two grenades into the front ends of the RZRs. They exploded and did backflips, crashing onto their tops. The shockwaves from the explosions sent the other men flying. They smashed down onto the pavement, knocking them out cold.

"Keep moving!" the voice from the helicopter said.

We ran full speed away from the warehouse, but Alonso's men had another surprise for us about 500 feet away. The double doors of a shipping container swung open and eight men came out, firing machine guns.

"Get back!" I yelled, yanking Leah behind a container.

"Stay back there!" the FBI ordered.

The chopper hovered over us and gunned down every single one of those guys.

"You're almost there! Keep going!" the voice said.

Leah and I took off, hand in hand. But then we saw a wall ahead of us.

"Josh! We're trapped!" Leah said, panicked.

I spotted a staircase on the outside of the warehouse. It went up to a balcony on the third floor that wrapped around the whole building.

"Not exactly! Come on!"

We flew up the metal stairs and ran along the balcony, the chopper hovering alongside us.

As we reached a corner, five of Alonso's men appeared with machine guns. I pointed my HK433 and was about to pull the trigger when the gunner in the chopper opened fire, killing them all.

"We've got you! Now keep moving!" the voice said.

We hightailed it around the corner and saw the red-and-blue flashing lights of a large convoy of police and FBI vehicles speeding toward the warehouse. The chopper disappeared around the corner of the building, and I didn't know where it was going.

Then another group of Alonso's men came up a staircase pointing their machine guns at us. We stopped in our tracks as I pointed my HK433 at them.

"Josh, behind us!" Leah screamed.

Five more men faced us, all of them holding machine guns. We were surrounded.

I pointed my HK433 at one guy and then another, and then another guy, but they just kept coming. One walked right up to me and pointed a knife into my face.

"Failed to save her again, huh, homes?" he said. "Here's what we're gonna do. We're gonna bring you both back to Alonso, he's gonna cut your hearts out, and he's gonna let you watch them stop beating."

I was just wondering where the chopper had gone when it circled around the building and approached us.

"Get down!" the voice yelled.

I punched Alonso's guy in the face, knocking him away from me, then pulled Leah to the floor. I lay on top of her as the gunner with the M249 opened fire, sending bullets flying across my back and taking out every one of those guys.

I lifted my head and saw the men lying around us in pools of blood. I pulled Leah up, and we looked at the chopper in relief. I gave the pilot a thumbs up.

In the distance we saw the headlights of another RZR speeding toward us. Juan was driving, Alonso beside him. They screeched to a halt, and Juan stepped out. He reached inside, pulled out a .50 caliber sniper rifle, and pointed it at the helicopter.

"Oh, God no! Pull back! Pull back!" I yelled at the helicopter. But it was too late. Juan fired and hit the tail rotor, causing the pilot to lose control. The chopper began to spin, smoke coming out of the tail.

I pointed my HK433 at Juan. He jumped back into the RZR, put it in reverse, and screeched away. I pulled the trigger, firing on full auto until the magazine was empty, but I didn't hit them, and they got away.

"Damn it!"

The chopper was still spinning, but the pilot was able to get it over the water, where both gunners bailed out. Then it came spinning back toward us, out of control!

"Josh!" Leah yelled.

The tail hit the side of a crane, breaking off. Then the chopper spun even faster toward us!

"Run! Run!" I yelled.

We ran down the balcony toward a staircase. Then I realized the helicopter was about to slam into the balcony. It was spinning so fast toward us that I knew Leah and I wouldn't make it running down the staircase. We would have to jump off the balcony.

"Leah, jump!" I screamed. I wrapped my arms around her, and we leapt forward. The chopper exploded into flames, and the balcony began to collapse beneath us.

"Come on!" I yelled. We got back on our feet and sprinted down the balcony as section by section fell beneath our feet. Then we jumped down onto a shipping container and rolled onto the ground.

"Are you OK?" I asked, turning to look at her.

"Yeah, I'm fine."

"Come on. We're almost out of here."

We ran along the outside of the warehouse until we reached a window, where I saw Alonso and Juan driving the RZR inside!

"Leah, stop!" I pulled her back.

Juan parked the RZR right next to a brand-new Jeep Grand Cherokee Trackhawk.

I realized I couldn't run away and hope the FBI would take care of these guys. I had to deal with them myself. These two were like cancer. If I didn't handle them, they'd just kept coming back.

I wracked my brain for a plan. Just then I saw hope: flashing red-and-blue lights from a convoy of police and FBI vehicles plus several helicopters coming through the gate.

"Oh thank God!"

I had to challenge Alonso and Juan, but I didn't want to take Leah with me.

"Leah, see those cops? Run to them, and find Agent Carter. He'll keep you safe."

"Josh, aren't you coming with me?"

"I can't! I have to deal with these two! Now's my chance to finish them off."

"Josh, come with me!"

"No! I've got to take them out, or we'll never be free."

"Josh!" A tear rolled down her check. "I don't want to lose you."

I pulled her to me, face to face. "I love you," I said, "and that's why I have to get rid of them by myself without you in harm's way."

She looked deep into my eyes and then hugged me.

"Find Agent Carter," I said. "Hurry."

Leah nodded, her head on my shoulder. She kissed me and then ran toward the cops.

I looked through the window and saw Juan jump into the Jeep's passenger seat. Alonso jumped into the driver's seat and fired up the engine. The LED headlights lit up.

I loaded another magazine into my HK433. I wasn't going to be merciful this time; that was for damn sure. I slid the window open, climbed inside, and ran into the path of the vehicle.

The men looked up, and their jaws dropped. Alonso shifted into drive, and I pointed my HK433 at him. He hit the gas, charging at me. I pulled the trigger, spraying bullets into the windshield. Juan and Alonso ducked under the dashboard. I kept firing until I ran out of bullets. Alonso slammed the Jeep right into me, sending me up onto the hood, my weapon flying through the air. I grabbed a windshield wiper arm with both hands. Alonso smashed through the garage door and made a hard left turn, nearly sending me flying off the hood. He made a beeline for the exit gate, doing about 60 mph, swerving left and right and trying to throw me off, but I held on.

"Enjoying the ride?" he yelled.

I had to make him stop, so I grabbed one of my Glock 17s and fired two shots through the windshield, but I missed him, as he ducked and zigzagged. The windshield shattered but held in place.

Alonso drove around a container and slammed on the brakes as a semi-truck pulled out in front of us. The Jeep spun out of control, and I flew off the hood, hitting the ground and tumbling to the curb, scratching up my face and arms. The Jeep hit a fence, but Alonso spun it around and came right back at me. As they approached, Juan leaned out his window and fired at me with his automatic G36C.

I lay as flat as I could. As Alonso raced away, I pointed my Glock 17 at him and fired, but I missed every time. I thought there was no hope, but then I spotted my car!

"Ha! You're not getting away that easily," I said.

I hopped into the GTO and started the engine.

"All of this! All of this, for one guy in jail!" I said as I shifted into first gear, spun my tires on the dirt, and chased after Alonso and Juan.

CHAPTER 28

was driving over 100 mph on a busy divided highway with heavy traffic in both directions. Helicopters hovered over me, with their bright lights nearly blinding me.

I came to a busy intersection, spun, and drifted onto another street. Two cars spun out of control to avoid me.

After a few miles, I saw LED lights that looked like Alonso's Jeep speeding toward me. They must have changed direction! As they drew closer, I saw their windshield was riddled with bullet holes, so it was definitely them.

I steered onto the opposite side of the road, driving head on toward Alonso. My plan was to get him to steer into the curb. I shifted into sixth gear and pushed the gas pedal to the floor. Seconds later, he did exactly what I wanted.

I drove past him, hit the clutch, and slammed my brakes, causing all four wheels to lock. I spun my car 180 degrees. Two SUVs driving in both directions spun out of control trying to avoid me.

Alonso went up onto the sidewalk, through a group of pedestrians, and back onto the street. I put the GTO in first gear, spun around, and raced after him.

When I finally caught up, I bumped into his rear bumper,

sending him flying forward. Then I did it again, harder. He swerved but recovered.

I drove alongside the Jeep and slammed into the passenger side—twice. My car wasn't much of a match because of its light weight.

As I hit it a third time, Juan leaned out the window, and pointed his G36C at me.

"Whoa!" I hit my brakes, and Juan fired at the front end of my car, shattering the headlights, putting holes in the hood, and cracking a side-view mirror.

I steered over behind the Jeep to take cover. Juan climbed into the Jeep's rear cargo area and fired through the back window, hitting my windshield. I ducked under the dashboard, slammed on the gas, and hit the Jeep hard, knocking the weapon out of his hands.

I pushed on my windshield with one hand until the glue that was holding it together gave out, and the glass fell out.

Alonso and I were overtaking car after car until we were about to go past a 2007 Cadillac Escalade EXT. He slammed into one of the Escalade's rear quarter panels, causing it to spin in front of me. I steered around it and nearly hit it before it spun into the curb.

Then he drove up to a 2006 Ram 1500 mega cab towing a trailer with two jet skis on it. Juan leaned out his window and threw a grenade onto the trailer. When it exploded, the trailer broke away and flipped, throwing both jet skis into the street. I missed one, but the other rolled into the back corner of my car, nearly causing me to spin out of control, but I managed to recover.

Alonso drove up a ramp to Interstate 710, and I was right on his tail. We were doing over 120 mph with the helicopters hovering over us.

Just then Juan climbed up through the sunroof with a semi-automatic grenade launcher and pointed it at me!

"Oh hell no!" I said, as I hard-steered to the left. The grenade flew past and hit the pavement right behind me.

His second shot barely missed my car and hit the divider, sending chunks of concrete all over the freeway.

Alonso careened onward, and I steered into the middle lane. Juan fired another grenade, and it went between a Ford Excursion and a Audi Q7 SUV right next to me. The explosion flipped the vehicles, and they barrel-rolled down the freeway.

I knew I had to keep my distance as long as Juan had that grenade launcher in his hands!

I was about to drive past a GMC Sierra crew cab. Juan fired, and the grenade hit the Sierra's rear end. The truck flew through the air and landed on its side.

Juan crawled back inside the Jeep.

I was hoping he didn't have any other weapons but that hope didn't last long. He came back out with a shoulder-fired rocket launcher!

"Seriously?" I groaned.

Juan didn't aim at me but a semi-truck towing a box trailer. The rocket separated them, and the trailer rolled onto its side right next to me. The truck exploded and careened toward me. I put the pedal to the metal and dodged it before it slammed into the concrete divider.

Alonso took an exit ramp, and I was right behind him as he approached a red light at a busy intersection. He flew up to the light, then hard-steered left. Several vehicles spun around, and drivers honked their horns.

I chased after him, hard-steering too. A shuttle bus driver coming in my direction blared his horn and tried to avoid hitting me. He swerved, then hit the curb and two parked cars.

"Sorry, dude," I said as I zigzagged down the road, trying to avoid crashes.

Alonso sideswiped an EcoSport, sending it spinning into the middle of the road, and I darted around it.

Suddenly, I saw red flashing lights. Guard gates were coming down at a drawbridge. That meant a large boat was coming.

Alonso hightailed it straight toward the bridge as it rose slowly. I was scared because I knew his Jeep had a better chance of surviving a jump over that bridge than my Pontiac. My suspension wouldn't take it.

Alonso drove up the inclining bridge. He made it to the tip, ramped off it, and landed perfectly on the other side.

I slammed on my clutch and brakes, locking all four wheels as I slid toward the drawbridge. It rose to the point where my car couldn't drive up it, and I couldn't climb it.

Alonso sped away, Juan looking back at me and laughing.

"Aargh!" I hit the top of my steering wheel with my fists.

A helicopter had arrived, hovering close to me. Two others followed Alonso. Sirens were approaching.

I had to think of something. I knew Alonso couldn't get too far from me because the road he was on only went in one direction for several miles. There were no other roads to turn on. It went straight to Interstate 5.

I looked at the navigation screen in my car and found a different route, but it meant doing a bit of off-roading.

"You aren't getting away that easy," I said.

I shifted into first gear and hit the gas. My tires screeched as they spun, and I shot down the road beside the river.

A few minutes later, I reached another drawbridge. This time I flew across it before it could rise. Then I zoomed ahead.

Soon, I got a view of the other road and the Jeep, but an empty train yard lay between Alonso, and me and I couldn't drive over the tracks. Down the road I saw a section that was paved. I'd just have to avoid getting hit by a train if one came by because the train yard was busy.

I steered off the road into a ditch, then smashed through a fence and hightailed it across the tracks until I made it to the other side of the train yard. I hard-steered and drove alongside an incline that was parallel to Alonso.

The incline was a problem, but if I could speed up and make my car airborne, I could slam into the side of Alonso's Jeep, causing him to crash. That would mean totaling my car—my baby. I'd had it for a long time. I had so many memories associated with it, especially with Leah. It was the best vehicle I'd ever had. But at that point, I had to go all out to stop Alonso and Juan from getting away from me.

I can't believe I'm gonna do this, I thought.

I shifted into the highest gear and careened alongside the divider.

"Oh Lord! Oh Lord!" I pleaded out loud.

I ramped up the incline. All four wheels lifted off the ground and landed on the side of Alonso's Jeep, causing it to flip sideways. Both of our cars barrel-rolled down the street over and over until I slammed into a lamppost. My car landed on its top on the highway, with me dangling upside down by my seatbelt.

Broken glass lay all over my headliner. Car parts were all over the road. My head hurt, but I was OK. I unbuckled my seatbelt and landed on the headliner.

The Jeep was also on its top. Juan and Alonso struggled free of the crumpled vehicle and limped onto the pavement, their faces bloody. Alonso leaned against the vehicle, but Juan began walking toward me, holding his G36C.

Traffic was backing up, and a few people got out of their cars to try to help, but when Juan opened fire on full auto, they ran back, threw their vehicles into reverse, and screeched outta there.

As Juan continued toward me, I pretended I was dead as I lay there on the headliner. I heard Juan's boots approach. He opened the driver's door, and I felt him put two fingers on my pulse. He looked to see if I was breathing, but I was doing my best to keep still. He lay his hand under my vest to see if my heart was beating.

"¿Está muerto?" ("Is he dead?") Alonso yelled.

"No lo sé," ("I don't know") Juan said as he took his hand off me.

I slightly opened my eyes and saw he was standing right outside my door.

"Dudo que esté vivo," ("I doubt he's alive") Juan said. As he turned his back on me, I decided to make my move.

I pulled a Glock 17 from my holster, cocked it, and put a bullet in the chamber.

"Quiero asegurarme de que este muerto antes de que nos vayamos. Si no, lo mataré aquí," Juan said. ("I want to make sure he's dead before we go. If not, I'll kill him right here.")

I pointed my Glock at him and pulled the trigger. The bullet went through his leg. Blood spurted everywhere.

"Aaaaaaah!" he screamed, losing his balance and nearly falling. His weapon fell to the ground, but he quickly recoiled and grabbed my Glock with one hand and my vest with the other. "You son of a bitch!" he yelled as he pulled me out of my car and onto the pavement.

"Take care of him!" Alonso yelled. "I'm getting out of here!" He pulled two weapons out of the Jeep and ran down the highway.

The next thing I knew, I was David fighting Goliath, a small person fighting a giant.

I grabbed the other Glock from my holster, but when I tried to point it at Juan, he wrestled me and banged my hands on the asphalt, knocking the weapon out of my grasp. He punched my face, pulled me off the ground, and threw me over him like a rag doll. I landed hard on my back on the undercarriage of my overturned car. Then he yanked me off the car, sending me rolling to the curb.

I was exhausted, dizzy, and in pain. But through my blurred vision, I saw him walking toward me with a knife and a big grin.

I summoned all the energy I could.

"You may have nine lives," he said, "but this time I'm gonna make sure you die on the last one you have."

I quickly got vertical and pulled a throwing knife out of my vest.

Juan swung his blade at me, but I pulled back. He swung again and again, barely missing my arm. I took two swings at him, putting a long, deep cut on his arm. The second time, he grabbed my hand and vest and threw me against a parked minivan. The glass shattered, and I left a big dent.

As I scrambled to my feet, Juan kicked my knife out of my hand, then kicked me in the face, knocking me flat on my back. I thought it was all over, 'cause he was a big dude. He stomped his boot on my chest and started pressing it down. I pounded on his leg as hard as I could, struggling to breathe. He moved his boot over the gunshot wound from earlier and stomped on it with all his weight.

"Aaaah!" I screamed and gulped for air, hoping someone would hear and come to help. *Where are those helicopters and sirens now that I need those guys?* I wondered. Then Juan kicked my side, knocking me onto my stomach. He grabbed my throat with one hand and lifted me off the ground with the other, like I weighed nothing. I took hold of his arm with both hands, but he was too strong for me. He started squeezing my throat harder and harder, cutting off my air. I thought I was going to pass out.

Then, he raised his blade. I reached for one of my throwing knives and stabbed it into his shoulder. Blood streamed down his arm, but he didn't seem hurt. He grinned. I couldn't believe it. He had so much muscle and such thick skin that he could take it.

I took another stab at him.

Juan chuckled. "That tickles," he said.

I slashed my knife across his face.

"Aaaaah!" He let go of my neck and dropped me flat on the ground, where I lay gasping for air.

"Did that tickle?" I asked.

Juan dropped his knife and threw both of his hands over his face, as he screamed in pain. Now, he had a long, deep, bloody wound.

He grabbed his G36C. I ran and rolled over the hood of a Pontiac Grand Am. He fired several shots at me and just barely missed.

He ran and hid behind a Kia Optima and fired on full auto through the Grand Am's windows, shattering the glass right over my head. I reached for my DP12 shotgun in the back of my vest, leaned over the Pontiac's roof, and fired two shots through the Kia, but I missed him. I fired again and missed.

I ducked below the Grand Am. Then I heard something land on its roof! It was a frag grenade! It rolled off the roof and landed right next to me, about to explode.

I took off, and when I got about 10 feet away, the grenade exploded, sending me flying off my feet. The force flipped the Grand Am onto its top, and it exploded into flames.

Juan threw another grenade, and it landed beside me.

"Really?" I ran and I hid behind a Dodge Journey before it exploded.

"Anything else you want to throw at me?" I yelled. Just then another grenade rolled beneath the Dodge.

"Seriously?" I fled before it went off, but the explosion threw the Dodge onto its side. Another vehicle up in flames!

I hid by a Mack dump truck and decided to throw some of my grenades at Juan, since he loved them so much.

I grabbed one from my vest, then pulled the pin. I came out from behind the truck and threw it at the Kia. The grenade exploded, and I saw the Kia do a front flip and erupt into flames.

Pointing my shotgun in front of me, I walked toward the vehicle, but I didn't see Juan. I couldn't get close to the car because of the intense heat from the flames, so I looked all around it. I didn't see his body anywhere. I wondered if he'd run down the road before the grenade went off.

I'd have to go look for him, but I would have to be cautious because this could be a trap with a surprise attack.

I grabbed my Glock 17s off the ground and put them in my leg holsters, keeping my DP12 in my hands. I looked down the road toward the traffic. Perhaps Juan was among all of the backed-up vehicles. I walked in between them. People were blaring their horns, and some were yelling. I ran down a row of cars and lay under the grille of a Mitsubishi Montero. The driver leaned his head out of the window.

"Hey? What the hell is going on?"

"Stay in your car!" I yelled.

I looked around the traffic and under the vehicles and even in the back of pickup trucks.

Suddenly, a machine gun fired at me! I took cover behind a Lincoln Navigator. The bullets shattered its windows. The driver was a woman. She started screaming. I ran and hid under the grille.

"Stay down! Get down!" I yelled, and she ducked under the dashboard. I saw Juan hiding at the rear of a Mustang about four vehicles ahead of me. He leaned over the driver's side and fired again. I ducked back under the Navigator's grille. Bullets shattered the side-view mirror and flattened the tires on the driver's side.

Some people abandoned their cars and ran, screaming.

I wanted to return fire, but I was surrounded by innocent people, and my only option was to shoot from a safe angle.

He kept firing. Then I heard a woman scream, "No! No!"

"Get out! Get out, bitch!" Juan yelled.

I saw him pull the driver out of the Mustang and hold her hostage behind it. I couldn't let him harm her.

I came out from behind the Navigator, pointing my DP12's green laser sight at Juan's head.

"What you gonna do, chico punk?" he yelled. "Come on, homes!"

"Let her go! I yelled.

"Come at me, white boy! What you gonna do, huh homes?"

"Let her go!" I yelled, keeping the dot on him. "I'm not joking!"

"Drop the gun, or I'll kill the bitch!" he yelled as the woman screamed and cried for help. "Stay the hell back!"

I didn't want to risk hitting the woman or anyone else.

Juan pushed her toward me, knocking her off her feet. He fired his G36C at me, and I jumped and hid by the grille of a Nissan Titan crew cab. I leaned over the driver side and decided to take a shot while praying that I wouldn't screw it up.

I pointed my DP12 at Juan's leg and pulled the trigger. The slug only nicked his leg, taking out a chunk of skin.

"Damn it!" he yelped. Then he limped and hid behind a Ford Edge.

The hostage woman crawled toward me. I ran to her. "Come on, ma'am! You're gonna be OK. Just come with me!"

Juan leaned over the Ford Edge. Before he could take a shot, I fired my DP12. It hit the Edge's rear quarter panel. Juan ducked back behind the vehicle.

I pumped my DP12 with another two slugs in both chambers. Then I grabbed the woman by her arm and pulled her behind cover.

"Come on!" I yelled. We hid at the grille of a Toyota Tundra crew cab just right before Juan fired his G36C at us.

"Stay down!" I yelled to the woman as I lay on top of her,

keeping her sheltered. After Juan stopped firing, I looked around the side of the Tundra and saw him running between cars, reloading his weapon.

"I'm sorry, ma'am, but I have to go!" I said. "You'll be OK. Just stay low until the police get here."

"Wait, you're not the police?" The woman asked.

"No. I'm just doing their job for them," I said.

I jumped up and ran along the backed-up traffic, trying to find Juan. A flurry of bullets flew past me, barely missing me. I hid at the grille of an Acura MDX, and Juan kept firing. I threw myself on the ground and began crawling to the Acura's passenger side.

"This is insanity!" I yelled and lay flat on my stomach.

"Having fun over there, perra?" Juan shouted.

I crawled to the rear of the Acura. When I got back on my feet and leaned against the rear panel, another stream of bullets came at me. One punched through the panel and hit my shotgun, shattering it and knocking it out of my hands.

"Agh! Damn it!" All I had now were my Glock 17s and 18s and not much ammunition.

I pulled out both 17s and leaned around the Acura. When I saw Juan appear from behind a Honda Pilot, I rapid-fired at him. He ducked and moved behind a Pontiac G8. He put his G36C over its hood and blind-fired at me.

"Scared, aren't you, white boy?" Juan said, laughing.

I leaned around the back of the Acura and rapid-fired both Glocks, until they ran out of bullets and the slides locked back.

"Damn!" I said. Juan continued firing at me, so I had to keep moving. I saw a semi-truck with a box trailer behind the Acura. Behind the truck was an Infiniti SUV. That's where I planned to run.

I darted as fast as I could, and Juan fired his G36C through the box trailer. As I sprinted toward the SUV, I released the empty magazines out of my Glocks. Then I reloaded my weapons with my last two magazines as I leaned up against the SUV. Thud! I heard something bounce on the roof.

As I ran, there was an explosion, and it threw the SUV upside down and sent me flying. I slammed into the windshield of a Ford Expedition, cracking it. I rolled off the hood and landed on the ground.

"It's a damn war zone out here!" I said, as I got back on my feet and ran and hid on the driver side of a Ford Escape.

Then everything went eerily quiet.

I leaned over the hood of the Escape, but I couldn't see Juan anywhere. I walked cautiously to the Pontiac and looked around it and beneath it. No Juan.

Now I was really scared.

Then I heard helicopters hovering nearby, but I didn't know if having them around was good or bad, and I hoped for their sake that Juan, as crazy as he was, didn't shoot them down.

I walked down the line of traffic. An elderly couple was sitting in a Mercedes Benz SUV.

"Did you see where he went?" I asked.

"Who are you?" the man asked through the window, afraid to roll it down.

"Your guardian angel, grandpa!" I said. "Where'd he go?"

"He went into that train yard," he said.

"Alright. Everything's gonna be fine. Just stay in your car," I told them. They looked afraid.

I wasn't sure how much longer I could keep fighting Juan. I was weak and getting low on ammunition, and I still had Alonso to deal with. But if I played it smart, I'd be OK.

In the train yard, I had to watch out for any speeding freight trains as well as Juan.

I kept my Glock 17s pointed in front of me as I walked between train cars. A locomotive slowly rolled past me. Then I walked across the tracks and between two boxcars.

I looked under every single train car, but I didn't see Juan. I was tired of playing hide-and-seek with him. It was getting old.

The empty part of the yard lay ahead. That was where freight trains might speed through at 70 mph. I would have to be extremely careful.

A small building came into view, and I wondered if he could be hiding in there. So, I jogged along the train cars. When I got to what appeared to be a storage house, I walked around the exterior. No Juan.

I looked through a window but didn't see him. What I did see was a lot of railroad equipment and a Chevy Silverado parked inside. *But he might still be in there,* I thought. I couldn't see everything yet.

A chill went down my spine, and every hair on my body stood on end, as I crept through a door, both Glocks in front of me. I walked very slowly around the equipment. I looked inside the Chevy Silverado and the truck bed. No Juan. I looked underneath it. Nada.

Then I heard a strange sound inside a cabinet behind me, like something was moving inside it. Keeping my weapons pointing at the cabinet, I walked over to the side of it. I twisted the knob, swung the door open, and a couple of rats jumped out!

"Agh! Damn rats!" I said. Just then the double doors of another cabinet on the other side of the building swung open, and Juan appeared, holding two automatic Mac 11s.

"Surprise!" he said and fired both of them at me.

I threw myself to the floor and crawled behind a stack of train rails.

When he stopped firing, I leaned around the rails and saw him hiding behind a forklift. I could just see the top of his head. I also could also see one of his Mac 11s.

"I see you behind there!" Juan said, laughing. "Scared, aren't you? You want my advice? You should really try dying. That's what sheep are supposed to do anyway."

I fired one of my Glocks, shattering Juan's weapon and injuring his hand.

"Aaaah! Son of a bitch!" he yelled as he threw himself on the ground. I rapid-fired at him, but he crawled back behind the forklift.

"Thanks for the advice," I said. Juan blind-fired his other Mac 11. I leaned back behind a stack of rails as the bullets flew past, nearly hitting me. Some were hitting the other side of the train rails, making loud pinging sounds that rang in my ears so badly that I could barely hear myself think.

Juan stopped firing. I leaned around the side of the rails and rapid-fired at him. He leaned back behind the forklift. That was when my worst fear happened—both slides on my Glocks locked back open. I was out of magazines!

"Damnit!" I said, as I crawled back behind the stack of rails and threw my weapons down. They were useless now. All I had were my Glock 18s, but I didn't have much ammunition left.

I heard a clanging sound coming from where Juan was. I wondered what he was doing.

Then something landed on top of the stack of rails. A moment later, a grenade rolled off a beam and landed right next to me.

I got to my feet and ran like there was no tomorrow. I headed for a window, but I didn't get far from the grenade before it exploded. It threw me into the air and straight out the window. A trail of fire followed me as I landed and rolled into the worst possible place—the middle of some train tracks at the busiest end of the yard. Debris from the building landed and all around me. The building was on fire.

I looked both ways and didn't see any lights from trains coming. It could have been worse. I could've landed in front of an oncoming train.

Juan walked toward me with his Mac 11. He stopped when he was about twenty feet away. Then he took the magazine out and dropped everything on the ground.

"I'm not gonna cap you where you lie. No, homes," he said. "That would be too easy. Too quick, ha ha ha. I wanna play with you first before you die. Make it more fun for me. Now get up."

He wanted a fistfight. I accepted his challenge. I was going to fight this dude who was 6 feet 6 inches and 250 pounds—all muscle.

My rage helped me get back on my feet as I looked Juan straight in the eyes.

I dropped my Glock 18s while preparing myself for a brutal beating. I was going to give Juan as much hell as I could.

We raised our fists at each other and started walking in a circle, closing in. Juan threw the first punch toward my face. I dodged it by an inch.

I threw my fist toward his face, and he dodged. I went back toward Juan, threw my fist at him two more times, but on the third time, he grabbed my fist and punched me in the nose with his other hand. While he was still holding my fish, he spun around, twisting my arm. Then he pulled me over his body, making me do a front flip. I landed on my back.

Before I could get on my knees, Juan kicked me in my side, throwing me flat on my back again.

"Ha, ha. Is that it? With all that anger you have? Get up!"

I climbed back on my feet, and Juan walked up to me again. I unleashed the beast in me and gave it to him. I kicked his kneecap inward. He went down onto his other knee. I jumped and kicked him in the chin, knocking him to the ground.

When he got back on his feet, I ran at him and side-kicked him on both sides like a ninja and punched the sides of his head. Then when he threw his fist at me, I did the most intense self-defense move I knew—which I never thought I could do. I grabbed his arm with one hand, punched him in the chin, and then threw my whole body off the ground. I wrapped my legs around his neck, used my body weight to pull him down to the ground, and then I pinned him down with his head between my feet. I twisted his arm until I heard something crack.

"Aaaaah!" Juan screamed as I kept twisting his arm until the cracking stopped. Then I let him go and got back on my feet. He kicked me right in the center of my chest, sending me back a few feet.

I hoped his arm was broken and that he'd be almost unable to do anything with it, but I couldn't have been more wrong. He reached for a baseball-sized rock and threw it at me. It hit me square in my forehead, knocked me over and sent me skidding back a couple of feet into a train rail. I was in so much pain that I almost couldn't move.

Then it got worse! I heard a train's horn in the distance. I looked up and down the tracks and saw the lights of a speeding locomotive barreling toward me. I could hardly move due to all the pain. I rolled off my back and onto my chest. Then I crawled off the tracks. But then Juan came up to me from behind and grabbed my throat, choking me. Then he grabbed my left arm, lifted me onto my knees, and held me right at the edge of the tracks. I knew he intended to throw me in front of the train.

"I'm done playing with you," he said. "Ah look at that. CSX is coming." The train blared it's horn again. "You're not gonna change the world fighting us. Why change it? It's great as it is because killing white boys like you brings satisfaction to us. Ha ha ha!"

The locomotive blared its horn. It was getting louder and closer. I was terrified. The ground shook as it sped toward me.

I tried beating on Juan's arm, but I couldn't even reach it. I could barely breathe. I was getting weaker.

Then I looked at his leg and remembered that I had shot it back when I was inside my car. If I stomped on his wound, that would hurt him and get him to release me. Then I'd put him on the tracks instead.

The lights from the train were swiftly approaching. The heart-stopping horn was getting louder and louder. I needed to hurry.

I raised my boot off the ground and slammed it down on Juan's foot.

"Aaaah!" He yelled and bent over, letting go of me. I quickly kicked his leg wound. Then I grabbed a throwing knife out of my vest, swung myself 180 degrees to face Juan, and slashed his throat. He gasped, and his eyes got big and wide as his blood spilled out of his throat like a mini waterfall. I grabbed his vest with one hand and stabbed him in the gut with my throwing knife, leaving the knife inside him. Then I moved him over to the tracks with him facing me. Only then did I finally respond to his question.

"You're right. I can't change the world. But you know what? Killing you is a good start."

I shoved him onto the tracks and quickly stepped back as the train roared in, annihilating Juan. The rush of wind from the speeding train almost blew me off my feet. Juan was finally gone. My heart was racing. All I could think was that I would hate to see what the front of that locomotive looked like. He may have survived a gunshot, he may have survived getting stabbed several times, and he may have even survived a bad car crash, but there was no way in hell that he could have survived getting hit by a 100-ton locomotive doing 80 mph.

I breathed a huge sigh of relief and turned around. Time to find my next and final target . . . Alonso.

"One down, one to go."

CHAPTER 29

picked up my Glock 18s and hurried to a construction site just down the road from where I crashed my car. That seemed to be the most likely place for Alonso to hide.

News helicopters still hovered over me, shining their spotlights.

A high-rise building was underway. The internal structure was in place, but there was no exterior. I saw equipment on each floor. A tower crane stood next to the building holding multiple steel beams by its lift cables.

I hopped over the fence and ran toward the building. A bullet hit the dirt beside my feet. It was followed by another bullet, and then a spray of bullets from a machine gun spattered the ground right beside me.

"Damn!" I jumped and hid behind a pile of steel beams. When the shots stopped, I looked over the beams and saw a fiery flash coming out of the barrel of Alonso's assault rifle. He was standing on the rooftop. He fired at me again, nearly hitting me in the head.

I couldn't hide behind those beams forever. I had to come out, and the building was about one hundred feet or so from me. I would have to run as fast as I could and try to avoid getting shot. Then I'd have to sprint up to the rooftop and fight off Alonso because all I had were my Glock 18s, which weren't for long-distance shooting. I took a deep breath and exhaled. Then I made a run for it.

Alonso fired at me as I zigzagged, avoiding the bullets hitting the ground around my feet until I made it into the building.

In the center of the building was a construction elevator. I ran to it, but it was locked. I would have to use the staircase all the way to the top. There were about ten floors. I raced up until I finally came to the last set of stairs that led to the rooftop. Now I had to be extremely careful. I climbed slowly, my Glocks in front of me. Eventually, I saw the pitch-black sky. Keeping my Glocks pointed up, I leaned against the concrete wall of the staircase and walked very slowly.

Heavy construction equipment was on the rooftop, and building materials were everywhere. Alonso could be hiding anywhere, and he knew I'd be coming.

Trying to keep hidden. I came to a large cement mixer, but I didn't see Alonso. Then I walked to a pallet of stacked concrete bags. A bullet flew at me and nicked the side of my leg.

"Aaah! Damn it!" I yelled as I sheltered behind the bags. Blood streamed through my pant leg.

"You just won't quit, will you?" Alonso asked from a distance. I leaned around the corner and saw him on the other side of a power generator. He was holding a Kriss Vector submachine gun, and he had an M72 rocket launcher strapped to his back. "You truly are pathetic, Joshua."

I held one of my Glocks over the top of the concrete bags and blind-fired a burst of shots. I leaned over the top of the bags and saw Alonso crouching behind the generator.

I rose up, pointed both Glocks at him, and fired. After the bullets hit the generator, he came out running. I continued firing on full auto until he hid behind a storage container.

My Glock 18s were out of bullets.

"Really? I exclaimed as I lay back behind the bags and reloaded them with my last two thirty-three-round magazines. A sudden volley of bullets hit the top of the bags, and some bullets flew right past me.

I leaned my head up over the top of the bags and waited for Alonso to appear. For a few seconds, I couldn't hear him. However, I could hear the helicopters above me. Alonso's silence was worrying me because he could have been hiding somewhere else and planning a sneak attack on me.

So, I laid back beneath the bags and turned on both red laser sights on the Glocks, so I could have more accuracy on shots within thirty feet. Then I stood up.

Out of nowhere, Alonso jumped over the bags and tackled me down to the ground. Then we fought hard to see who could shoot the other point-blank in the face first.

While Alonso had me pinned to the ground, he pointed his Kriss Vector right into my face. I pushed the barrel away from me right before he pulled the trigger and fired a burst of bullets into the ground next to my head.

I shoved him off me into the concrete wall, then pointed both Glocks at him. He ducked right before I pulled the triggers, my bullets burying themselves into the wall.

Then he ran into my chest, tackling me and pointing his weapon into my face once more. I smacked the barrel away before he pulled the trigger. Then I pointed a Glock in his face, but he grabbed my arm and pulled me right over him. I landed on the other side of him.

We both got back on our feet, and I aimed my weapons at him again. He pushed the pistols out of his face before I fired a burst of bullets. He pointed his Kriss Vector right into my face again, and I shoved it away before he fired.

I hit Alonso in his face twice with the Glocks. We kept alternating, pointing our weapons at each other and shoving them away. Eventually, he grabbed my vest with one hand, spun me around, and wrapped his arm around my neck. I back-kicked his kneecap as hard as I could.

"Aaah!" he yelled as he buckled over in pain. I elbowed him in the face, grabbed his vest with both hands, and rolled him over my back. He landed hard on the ground in front of me.

I was going to finish him off, but he struggled onto his feet. We both pulled our triggers at the same time. Alonso's Kriss Vector clicked over and over, and both of my Glocks clicked too. They were empty. Now I was completely out of ammunition.

Alonso kicked me in the chest, sending me back a few feet. I tripped over a concrete bag and landed on my back.

I had to think quickly. Now all I had to defend myself were the last throwing knives in my vest.

Alonso took a few steps toward me and tossed his weapon away since it was useless to him now. He unstrapped the M72 off his back and set it down by the pile of concrete bags.

"That's alright," Alonso said, as he pulled a razor-sharp knife out of his holster. "I'd rather slice you open anyway."

I got back onto my feet, took my vest off, pulled out a throwing knife, and prepared to have a blade fight with him.

We started moving in a circle, closing in on each other while holding our blades level with our faces. When we were about ten feet apart, I darted at him, swinging my knife left and right, over and over again. He dodged every time, as though he knew exactly where I was going to swing.

Alonso swung at me a couple of times and nearly slashed my hand. Then he almost slashed my cheek. We swung our knives at each other at the same time, and our blades hit, creating sparks.

I punched Alonso in the face and then kicked him in the chest, shoving him back. He tripped over a shovel and landed on his back. I darted at him as he got back on his feet and swung my knife at him multiple times, but he dodged every time.

After I nearly cut his arm, he punched the side of my head, then spun around and swung his knife, putting a deep, nasty cut across my cheek.

"Aah!" I took several steps away from him, holding my hand over the cut. When I pulled my hand away, it was covered in blood. I didn't know how much more abuse I could take. I was getting pretty faint. Luckily, so was Alonso.

He ran at me and kicked me in the chest, knocking me onto the concrete floor. He charged and jumped in the air with his blade held high, ready to stab me when he landed. I rolled out of his way, then spun around and slashed him on his cheek.

He wiped the blood off his face and gave me a look of rage. Then he charged, tackled me, and pinned me against the wall, holding my arm so I couldn't use my knife.

He was about to stab me, but I grabbed his wrist and pushed the knife back with all my might. The tip of the blade got closer and closer to my eye.

"How about I cut your eyes out? Sound good to you?" Alonso asked. "Because it does to me, ha ha!"

I lifted my foot and kneed his gut, which made him let go of me. Then, I sliced his ear.

"Aaaaah!" Alonso howled.

"Yeah. I 'hear' what you're saying," I said.

He came at me again. I ducked, and he swiped the cinder block wall with his blade, creating sparks.

I grabbed his vest, spun around, and threw him into the wall.

Then I swung at him, and he ducked. My blade sparked against the wall too.

He tackled me and wrapped his arms around my waist. We both tripped over a stack of bricks. In the scuffle, I dropped my knife, and it landed right next to him. He grabbed it, so now he had two knives, and I had nothing. Then I spotted a crowbar in a storage bin.

Alonso charged, swinging both knives like a ninja, but I dodged and swung at him with my crowbar, though I missed him the first two times. On the third swing, I hit his hand, knocking the knife out of it. Then I swung and hit him in his shoulder, knocking him into the side of a dumpster. He hit it so hard that he dropped his other knife.

Well, that wasn't as hard as I thought it would be.

As he got back on his feet, he chuckled and smirked, clapping a couple of times.

"Come on, bitch," he said. "Give me all you have."

"Batter up!" I said as I swung my crowbar. But I didn't hit Alonso; I hit the dumpster, leaving a big dent.

I dropped the crowbar and started punching Alonso in his stomach over and over again. When I went to hit him in the face, he ducked under my fist, and I punched the steel storage container instead.

"Ow!" I cried, wincing.

He punched me in the stomach, then stomped his foot into the gunshot wound on my left leg.

"Aaah!" I yelled as I got down on one knee. Then Alonso grabbed the crowbar and swung it at me. He hit me in the side of my head, and I fell to the ground. I heard ringing in my ears, and I felt a massive, painful headache. I lay flat on my back, my hands over my head. Then I turned onto my side and saw Alonso drop the crowbar and walk over to grab his RPG. I knew what he was going to do next, and I sure as hell was not going to let that happen.

I got back on my feet and jumped onto his back, grabbing the rocket launcher, then pulled him down to the ground, trying to wrestle it out of his hands. I kept my eyes on the trigger.

I finally got it, but Alonso kicked it out of my hands. It flew away, spinning vertically. When it hit the ground, facing up, it went off, releasing the rocket with smoky fire. It hit the operator's cab of the tower crane next to the building, causing a massive explosion and destroying that part of the crane. The entire top section started coming undone.

"Oh God no!" I cried, staring in disbelief. This was not good at all. The top of the crane broke off the tower and began falling onto the roof, along with about twenty tons of steel beams it had been holding. That part of the crane already weighed about eighty tons. So, one hundred tons of steel were coming our way, and the entire building was about to come down.

Alonso and I ran side by side from where the crane was about to land. The beams and crane crashed down with such an impact that they shook the whole building and sent us flying. The crane smashed through the roof and every level, all the way down to the ground. It sent up a huge cloud of dust, so we could barely see each other. The building continued to shake, and then the rooftop under us started cracking and collapsing all around us.

Large sections of the roof began falling. I was horrified, but I had to keep an eye on Alonso. I couldn't believe I was dealing with a high-rise disintegrating under my feet as well as a psychopath who wanted to murder me. Which was the priority?

Alonso grinned and came toward me. "You know something, Josh? People like you don't deserve heaven. You're about to learn that."

Instead, he was about to learn that the huge hole in the roof behind him was expanding closer and closer toward his feet. Now I could finally finish him off. Seconds later, he looked down at his feet in shock as they teetered on the edge. I raised my foot and kicked him in the center of his chest, knocking him backwards. He fell down to the next level.

I looked through the dust and saw him lying amidst the debris. But surprisingly, the fall didn't kill him. I saw him struggling to get up. He looked up at me. and we locked eyes.

A loud bang went off right next to me, and I saw that one of the five-ton beams was sliding off the roof and was about to fall through the gaping hole. The best part was, Alonso was lying in the exact spot where the beam was going to land!

I walked over to it and looked down at Alonso, grinning.

"You're right!" I yelled. "I don't deserve heaven. But you sure as hell don't either!"

I kicked the side of the beam as hard as I could and then watched with relief and satisfaction as it went down over the edge, straight as an arrow to its target, Mr. Alonso.

"Aaaaaaaaah!" Alonso's eyes nearly popped out of his head when he saw what was coming. He screamed as though that would save him. The beam pierced him, killing him instantly, and then smashed through that floor and kept falling through the other levels all the way down to the ground.

I couldn't believe I was finally rid of him. I took a big breath and straightened up, but I wasn't out of the woods yet. I was standing on the roof of a building that was collapsing, and it was collapsing fast!

Time to leave!

I only had moments to figure out how to escape the roof before it collapsed completely under my feet. My problem was that I was ten stories up. What was I supposed to do, jump? Even if that had been my only option, it would have been better than the way Alonso met his demise.

I ran from the collapsing sections of the roof to the other side of the building, where I saw the flashing red-and-blue lights of the police and FBI cars. Helicopters continued to hover.

I assessed my options. I knew I wouldn't survive jumping off a hundred-foot building. I looked over to the side and saw a wooden platform for construction workers to climb like a staircase, but the part of the crane that fell on the roof was blocking my way to the platform. Also, the top of the platform was on fire.

I would have to run and jump off the edge and land on the platform. *I've already been outside a skyscraper a thousand feet in the air jumping onto a balcony,* I thought, *so I should be able to do this.*

I ran back a few steps, took a deep breath, and then raced toward the edge. I leapt to the platform, grabbed a railing, and dangled over the side. The platform shook violently.

When I'd descended two levels, it started shaking harder. I stopped and grabbed the railing with both hands. I looked up and saw that the roof had completely collapsed and the rest of the building was coming down as well.

"Oh Lord!" I said, as the platform started falling apart too.

The news helicopters were backing away from the building, which didn't make me feel any better!

A large chunk of concrete fell and broke through the boards right next to me. Now, I couldn't go down any farther. I was stuck. Then, the whole platform started tilting away from the building and began plummeting toward the ground, where all the cops were running for safety.

I thought I was going to die and that I better say my last prayer. By the time the platform was at a forty-five-degree angle, I couldn't hold on any longer because of the weight of the platform. I lost my grip and went airborne.

The building collapsed, and the platform crashed down on top of several cop cars. I hit the ground with a hard thump. Then debris and dust rained down on me. A sheet of plywood hit me in the head, knocking me out cold.

I opened my eyes an untold number of minutes later and realized I was buried under construction debris. Everything I was hearing was an echo. I heard Leah screaming for me. She sounded close by.

"Josh? Josh? Where are you?" Then it sounded like she was talking to the others. "Come on, help me find him!"

I was badly hurt and could hardly move because of the weight on top of me. I thought my right leg had broken in the fall.

I was so weak that I couldn't speak. My lungs were full of dust, and my throat was sore from breathing it. I was gradually able to move the sheet of plywood off me, along with a small chunk of concrete. Then I slowly climbed out from under the platform and was eventually free outside. As I inhaled, I began to cough so violently that I nearly vomited. All around me was a cloud of dust. I couldn't see more than about thirty feet. I figured I looked like Casper the ghost. At least the echoing stopped, and my full concentration returned.

I stood up and limped around the wreckage, trying to find Leah. I was in so much pain that every step hurt.

"Josh! Can you hear me?"

Near a police Ford Explorer smashed by the platform, I saw Leah. She was picking up debris and throwing it away, digging and trying to find me.

"JOSH! Where are you?" She started crying, looking up at the sky. "Please! Please! You can't leave me!"

I grinned, and then I got her attention.

"Hey, beautiful."

She turned around, and when she saw me standing there in the flesh, she put her hands over her mouth and gasped.

"Josh!" Her face broke into a big smile, and she ran full speed toward me. When she reached me, she threw her arms around my neck, and we hugged like we hadn't seen each other in years. She squeezed me so tight it hurt. But I didn't care because I was so happy to have her back safe and sound and in my arms.

While she had her head buried in my shoulder, crying, I was also tearing up with joy. I had prayed and prayed to God for her protection. It looked like he had listened to me after all. Praise the Lord for that.

Leah looked into my eyes, kissed my lips, and smiled.

"Hey, I'm not going anywhere," I said. She grinned and put her hand on my cheek.

"Josh?" Agent Carter said from behind me. Leah and I unwrapped our arms, and I turned around and saw him and several other cops and FBI agents. "Hey, he's over here! We found him!" he yelled to the others.

When Carter reached me, he noticed how badly hurt I was. My clothes were torn up, I had gunshot wounds on my leg and cuts and bruises all over my body and face. "You look rough, buddy."

"I feel worse than I look," I replied.

Carter held his smartphone to his ear. "Get a medic up here ASAP! Our subject is badly hurt!" Then he hung up and nodded at me. "Can you walk?"

"Sorta," I said. "I'm limping, but I can get around."

"We'll get you patched up. Come with me."

CHAPTER 30

I t was over; it was all finally over. I wasn't afraid for my life or Leah's life anymore. I felt free from all the negative, and I felt so much joy and pride for doing what I'd done for my girlfriend. The day Leah left for college, I told her that I would always be there for her. I had kept my word. I didn't run away, thinking of my own safety. I took the law into my own hands and protected the ones I loved.

Alonso's operation was over. Everything with his name on it was finished. His father was in prison, and he wasn't going anywhere. He was there to stay, and he would rot within those walls.

As for all the news channels who were talking about me being wanted for the murder of those cops who tried to kill me, when I went on my phone and looked up all of the trending news, every news organization was saying I was the victim the whole time. I definitely felt better seeing those headlines because now I could go out in public without people thinking I was a criminal.

By 2:30 a.m. I was sitting on the back bumper of an ambulance holding an ice pack to my head while a paramedic cleaned blood off my skin and bandaged my wounds.

Leah was sitting next to me with her arms wrapped around me and her head on my shoulder.

"I don't think I'll be letting go of you for a while," she said.

"Ha, ha. You don't have to," I replied.

My phone dinged. It was the new verse of the day.

"What's the verse for today?" Leah asked.

I smiled. "Look at this." Leah looked at my phone screen. It was Psalm 20:8, "They are brought down and fallen, but we are risen, and stand upright."

"Wow, I'll say." We both chuckled.

"You know what the verse was yesterday?" I asked. "James 4:17, 'For he who knows the right thing to do but doesn't do it, for him it is sin.' I read that verse yesterday morning before I went to look for you. I knew that verse wasn't a coincidence. It was the Lord telling me something."

Leah kissed my cheek. "So . . . I was talking to Agent Carter . . ." Leah took her head off my shoulder and looked into my eyes. "You really did all the things he said you did? Like, sneaking into my dad's office and rappelling out of the building?"

I was kinda hoping Leah wouldn't know about the stuff I did because I didn't want to scare her any more than I already had. But the cat was out of the bag now.

"Yeah, I did," I said, nodding.

"You went to my dorm room, where they thought you shot those cops?"

"Yup."

"The Mercedes Benz dealership?"

"It's all true. I did everything you saw on the news. The gas station, the car chase, I blew up that oil complex, everything."

Leah shook her head and then chuckled. "Wow."

I grinned. "I was literally at the point of tearing the city down to find you, and I wasn't gonna think twice about anything."

She shook her head, grinning at me. "Wow. You literally went through hell and you never gave up."

I grinned and then I put my hand on her cheek. "I was never gonna give up, Leah."

"Josh?" It was Karen. She was walking over with Frank. Karen hugged me so tight that it hurt. I didn't want to complain though.

"Josh, I'm so glad you're OK!"

"Thanks Karen. Hi Frank."

She kept squeezing me tighter.

"Karen, easy—easy please!"

"Oh, I'm sorry!" She let go of me instantly. "I'm sorry!"

"It's fine."

"Can you walk OK?"

"Not really. I'm gonna be pretty sore for a while."

"Aww, Josh you poor thing." Karen kissed my forehead. "You look sore."

Frank stepped out from behind her with his hands in his pockets, looking like he was trying to find the words to say. I could only imagine how he was feeling, standing in front of me after the last time we talked—I mean *fought*. He had a bandage over his nose from when I punched him.

"Hey, Josh," he said with a grin. "How ya feeling, buddy?"

"Hey Frank," I said. "I'm sore."

"You look like it," he said, chuckling.

"You um . . . you look a little sore yourself."

Frank grinned and nodded. We both felt awkward.

"Frank . . . um . . . look . . . about what happened back at the house, I really am sorry."

"Actually, Josh. It's . . . um . . . Karen and I talked, and she made me realize a lot of things shortly after you left. If anybody should be sorry, it's me. I've been nothing but disrespectful to you this whole time, and I never even took a minute to listen to what you had to say. I've treated you so poorly ever since the day I met you. After everything that's happened today, I realize how much you really do love Leah and Karen. When I first met you, I thought you were just a punk with a crotch rocket."

Leah and Karen chuckled because they knew that was true. Even I had to laugh.

"But I was wrong about you," Frank continued. "You aren't nearly what I thought you were. There's a lot more to you than what meets the eye. I never should have judged you, but that's what I've been doing all these years, thinking you were just going to be a disappointment for my daughter. She loves you with a passion, and you obviously love her. Karen adores you too."

I grinned at Frank, thinking he was getting ready to say that he loved me too.

"Do you love me?" I asked cheekily.

"I'm getting there," he said. "You've always been nice to me and my family, and you've always been there for us. So . . . yeah. I guess I'm saying it . . . I love you Josh."

He said it! He said! For the first time ever! He legit said he loves me!

"You're making me blush," I said, laughing. Leah and Karen laughed too.

"You love me," I said. "You actually love me. Now give me a hug." I opened my arms for him.

"I'm good."

"Nope! Nope! You said the L word. You gotta do it."

"How about a handshake?"

"Dude, I risked my life, my young life. You can do this for me. Besides, after all I've just gone through, I kinda need it."

"Dad, come on, really?" Leah said.

Finally, Frank caved. He walked over and put his arms around me. I did the same, and he hugged me for the very first time ever. It felt great.

"Awww, you do love Josh! I knew it!" Leah said. Frank unwrapped his arms.

"We all love you," Karen said as she kissed my cheek.

"Excuse me? Josh?" It was Agent Carter. Everyone turned toward him as he approached with two other cops. "Hey, how ya feeling, man?"

"I'm doing fine."

"Your honor," Carter said, turning to Frank, "do you care if I have a minute with Josh?"

"Go ahead," Frank said. "Josh, we'll be over at the car whenever you're ready."

"OK."

Leah kissed my lips and then walked away with her parents. This was going to be another awkward conversation because Agent Carter and I weren't exactly on good terms either.

"Josh, I want you to listen to what I have to say, and I want you to listen good. I have been with the Federal Bureau of Investigation for forty years, and I'm obviously not far from retirement, but never in my career have I ever dealt with someone like you. You know I'm in full authority to arrest you for everything you've done today, and by *everything* I mean you have a long rap sheet on you." Agent Carter shook his head. "But I'm not going to do it. Let me explain why. I was young and in love when I was your age, and I know that if I were in your shoes, I would've taken action the same way you did. Every civilian I've come across stands aside and expects us to take care of their problems for them, but you on the other hand, you actually did the impossible. You took the law into your own hands, risking your own life, fighting bad people to save your girlfriend. Not only that, you nearly destroyed half the city. I've seen crazy stuff in my time, but you gave everyone one hell of a show."

"I thought so too," I said.

"When you and I spoke on the phone earlier, I mentioned that we had arrested a few of our own men. They were on Alonso's payroll, giving him information about you behind our backs. I looked into the shooting back at the college, where we thought you shot that cop. I recovered the body cams off the cops, and they showed us everything that really happened. That one cop shot himself because he knew he was done when you got to him. Same thing back at the gas station when those two other guys tried to kill you."

"I'm sorry your guys turned out that way," I said.

"I'm sorry too, Josh," Carter said. "I was wrong about you in every way. What can I say? I'm sorry everything went this way for you. It turns out that you were innocent this whole time. I hope there are no hard feelings."

I grinned at him. "We're good," I said, and we shook hands

He smiled. "Well, after everything you've done, you are one crazy bastard, that's for damn sure."

I chuckled. "I didn't know I had it in me," I said.

Carter handed me his card. "Me and the guys have always got your back if you ever need us at all. You take care of yourself, Josh, OK?"

"I will. Thanks for your help."

Carter walked away.

"Have a good one, kid," one of the other men said as they walked away with him.

"Thank you," I replied.

In the distance, I saw Leah, Karen and Frank standing outside their Range Rover.

I slowly got off the bumper of the ambulance, and Leah ran up to me.

"So, what did he say? Is everything OK?"

"Yeah, everything's fine. We were just talking about everything that happened. We're good."

"For a second I thought he was going to put you in handcuffs."

"No. Everything's fine. Especially right now."

Leah grinned and put her arms around my neck. I put mine around her back, and she kissed me. We closed our eyes. A few seconds later, I opened my right eye and looked over her shoulder. Karen and Frank were watching us.

I knew Karen was silently "awing." Frank, on the other hand, appeared grossed out and tried to look away. It's a good thing Leah and I didn't grab each other's butts while we were playing tonsil hockey because that would have made Frank puke everything he'd eaten over the past week.

Finally, we unlocked our lips and hugged.

"I think it's time we go home," I whispered. She nodded, her head resting on my shoulder.

"I agree," she replied. "But first you need to get yourself to the hospital and get patched up 'cause you really need it. We'll follow you. The ambulance will take you there."

CHAPTER 31

O ne week later I was finally able to go home without fearing for my life and trying to figure out how to save Leah. It was so nice to have no stress. I hit my bed and slept for more than twelve hours while being on some heavy medications that the hospital gave me. It felt amazing. I didn't go back to work for a while because I was too injured. The doctor at the hospital wanted me to take a month off to recover. I didn't complain because after what I'd been through, I felt I deserved it. Leah is also taking a couple semesters off from school to readjust until she feels ok to go back.

I was sitting on my couch with my Apple MacBook on my lap looking at funny memes about me on social media. I'd become famous for fighting all those bad guys while saving Leah. People were loving me to death. A lot of the memes were romantic, about Leah and me. Most of them were funny, of course.

I was also shopping on cargurus.com for a replacement vehicle, seeing as I had totaled my GTO. I was still sad about it seeing as it had sentimental value.

My doorbell rang, and I heard Leah's voice.

"Josh, babe, you home?" She cracked the door open.

"Come on in, Leah."

She walked into the living room wearing black leather boots over white jeans with a gray T-shirt. Her long hair was down.

"Hey, cutie," she said as she sat down next to me and kissed my lips.

"How you doing, honey?"

"Whatcha looking at?" Leah asked, putting her head on my shoulder.

"I'm looking at stuff that people have been posting about me on Facebook, Instagram, and everywhere else."

"What kind of stuff? I hope nothing mean."

"No. Actually, people are supporting me. People have been making memes about me, and they're hilarious. Look at this one." It said, "When your girl says she can't wait to see you home," and it showed a video from one of the news choppers of me speeding down the highway in my GTO. Leah chuckled at it. "Here's another one." It showed a picture of the president saying, "The criminals on our streets must be taken care of," and a picture of me saying, "Yes, sir!"

Leah laughed "That's a good one!"

"This is my favorite one right here," I said as I pulled it up on my screen. It showed a picture of a group of thugs saying, "We ain't scared of nobody," and it showed me saying, "Boo," followed by another picture of the thugs running, screaming, and crying.

Leah laughed. "You should post those and tag me in them."

"I will. People out there are funny."

"Yeah, they are. I needed a good laugh like that today."

"How are you feeling?"

"I'm doing better. How about you?"

"Better too. I'm not as sore as I was earlier, and I can walk better too. I've been car shopping today. I found a few nice cars that I'm gonna go look at. I saw a 2009 Nissan 370Z, a 2010 Dodge Charger

SRT, and a 2016 Hyundai Genesis 3.8 Ultimate with pretty low miles and well maintained.

Leah grinned. "I'm really sorry about your car, Josh. I know how much you loved that thing."

"Hey, I can always replace a car. I just can't ever replace you." Leah kissed my lips and hugged me. "I'm leaning more toward the Hyundai Genesis," I said, "'cause it's newer, and I think it's a good-looking car. You wanna come with me to look at it?"

Leah unwrapped her arms. "Actually, Josh um, hold on for a second about looking at a car."

"Why?"

My front door opened, and to my surprise, Frank and Karen walked into the living room.

"Oh, hi guys!" I said.

"Hi, Josh, how are you feeling?" Karen asked, as she hugged me and kissed my forehead.

"I'm doing good," I said as I put my laptop aside and Leah and I got up off the couch. "This is a surprise."

"Yeah, well, Karen wanted to see you," Frank said.

I grinned at Frank. "How you doing?" I asked.

"I'm fine. How are you, buddy?" He came over and gave me a hug.

"Oh another hug! He's getting soft, ladies," I said. Karen and Leah laughed.

Frank grinned. "Hey, Josh, there's a reason why all of us are here."

"Is everything OK?" I asked.

"Everything's fine," Frank said. "Look, um . . . you risked your life to save my daughter. It cost you a lot of money to do that. It also cost you a vehicle that you loved. Karen brought up the idea of doing something for you, and I wanted to do something too. So, we have something for you."

I looked at Karen, then at Leah and back at Frank. All of them were smiling at me.

"What's up?" I asked with a smile.

Leah came up behind me and put a blindfold over my eyes while giggling, and Karen grabbed my hands.

"We'll walk you outside," Frank said, and then Karen started pulling me toward the front door, and Leah kept her hands on my shoulders. I felt us go through the door. We walked outside, and we all stood in my driveway in front of my garage.

Karen and Leah giggled behind me.

"Alright, on the count of three," Leah said.

"One, two three, surprise!" they yelled, and Leah took the blindfold off my eyes.

"Oh my God!" I shouted, bursting with joy. "A brand-new Ram 1500!" Leah, Karen, and Frank started laughing.

That's right! My surprise was a new Ram 1500 with the limited trim, which was the fully loaded luxury package. On the hood of the shiny, new truck was a giant white bow and a poster on the windshield that said, "Thank you son <3."

"Are you serious? Is this for me?" I ran over to the truck and examined it.

"It sure is!" Karen said.

It was a beautiful truck with Red Pearl paint, twenty-two-inch polished rims, LED headlights and taillights, chrome door handles, towing mirrors, and front and rear chrome bumpers. It was a 4WD with a 5.7 liter V-8 Hemi engine, and it had air suspension. The bed had a spray-in bed liner, and it also had built-in storage compartments. "OMG! It's beautiful!" I said.

"We were going to get you a new sports car," Frank said, "but I thought every man should have his own truck."

"Wow! It's the limited trim too! This is the nicest one you can get!"

"Only the best for you, Josh," Karen said.

It didn't matter what make or model it was. I was just so happy to have a free vehicle, especially from Leah's parents. I touched the truck's hood and then walked back over to Karen and Frank, tearing up.

"Thank you so much!" I said.

"Aww, come here!" Karen said I hugged her and then Frank.

"I can't believe you guys did this for me," I said as I wiped my eyes. "I seriously can't."

"You deserve it, Josh," Frank replied. "After everything you did to save Leah, this is the least we can do."

It was such an amazing feeling. I even started feeling like I couldn't accept the truck because of how much it cost. A Ram 1500 with the limited trim cost just shy of $70,000.

I looked at the truck and then back at Frank and Karen, shaking my head. "Guys, I can't take that truck. It's too expensive."

"Josh, look," Frank said, putting his hands on my shoulders. "I know you didn't have it easy growing up, with your parents giving you up at birth and then never really having a home, living in orphanages. You never had a family to turn to for help. When Leah met you and invited you over to our home, I didn't think much of you. Five years later, you're still here, and ever since day one, you've shown nothing but love, patience, understanding, and compassion for her. You've also done the same for Karen and me. I'm sorry it took me five years to realize that."

A tear rolled down my cheek, and I wiped it off. I couldn't believe Frank was saying such nice things to me after all these years. I had begun to suspect he didn't have a heart. Now I was seeing a whole different side to him. Being scared must have scared him straight—either that or my punching him in the nose knocked something into place.

"I always wondered if God would bring a great guy for Leah, and He definitely didn't disappoint," Frank said. "Would I buy an expensive truck for my daughter's boyfriend? No, I wouldn't, but I would for my son." Frank smiled. "And you are my son. You're also part of this family."

He hugged me, and I hugged him too.

"I love you, son."

After he said that, I held him tighter, feeling like I was holding my actual father.

"I love you too," I said.

"Aww, I can't resist! I want in!" Karen said. She came over and hugged the two of us.

"Neither can I!" Leah said, joining in.

While Leah, Karen, and Frank hugged me, I felt like I'd finally found the one thing I'd been missing my entire life: a family. After so many years of not having one, I felt like my heart had finally settled down from heartache and depression, as if it had finally found a home. I felt at peace with myself and with God.

Finally, we all unwrapped our arms.

"I hope you enjoy that truck," Frank said. "Guys will be jealous of you."

"Ha, I can see it now," I said. I looked at Leah and then took her hand. "How about we take a drive?"

Leah smiled. "Sounds good."

We walked toward my new wheels.

"Hey, Josh," Frank said.

We stopped in our tracks and turned around.

"You're forgetting something."

At first, I didn't know what he was talking about. Then he held up the key fob for the truck. He clicked on it and remote started the V-8 engine, then tossed the fob to me. "Go have fun. The gas tank's full."

I opened the door for Leah as the retractable running boards came out, and Leah stepped into the cab.

I sat in the driver's seat and looked around the luxurious interior. I couldn't believe this was really happening to me. "Wow! I can't get over how nice this truck is!" I said.

She grinned. "It sure is."

The interior was black with heated and cooled leather seats, a twin-panel sunroof, an electric rear sliding window, a twelve-inch touchscreen display stereo, and a full center console. The truck had every bell and whistle available.

"So, where should we go?" I asked.

"Hmm . . . I think I've got an idea," she said with a smile.

I laughed. "I think I know what you're thinking," I said. I lowered all four windows and then slid open the back window and the sunroof. Then I put the electronic gear shift in reverse and backed out of the driveway as Frank and Karen waved.

Leah loves the beach, so Santa Monica was our destination. We arrived as the sun was setting.

I raised the truck's air suspension all the way up and parked on the sand with the front end of the truck facing the ocean.

I lay on my back on the truck's hood with Leah lying on top of me. She wrapped her arms around my neck, and I wrapped mine around her back, and we kissed. We often used to do that on my GTO or on her Honda Accord, but it was our first time doing it on a luxury truck. As long as I had her in my arms, I didn't care what I was lying on.

Leah smiled as she looked into my eyes. "So, you love your new truck?"

"Yes, but I love you even more," I said and kissed her lips.

She chuckled. "You look good driving it."

"I feel good driving it."

"I bet. You really are amazing, Josh. You weren't kidding."

"About what?"

"Remember the day I left for school? You said you would always be there for me. You really meant it."

I put my hand on her cheek. "I did, and I always will."

She smiled and kissed me again. We spent the rest of the evening in each other's arms, holding each other tight.

After everything that happened with Leah getting kidnaped, I couldn't help but be reminded that we Christians are suppose to love our enemies. I was very well aware that I killed multiple people. I'm not proud of that and I never will be. I didn't know what killing felt like until I had to pull the trigger on someone. And I didn't know what evil was until it stared into my eyes. Either though I saved Leah, I was still traumatized after experiencing all of that. I knew it was self defense when I shot all those men that tried to kill me but it still didn't feel good after taking their lives and it was a emotional feeling that I wouldn't wish on my worst enemy. Unfortunately I had to learn the hard way that when you take someone's life, it stays with you.

While growing up, I always wondered what my life would be like. I had prayed for an answer to that question for as long as I could remember. I finally got my answer when I met Leah and her parents five years ago.

That family sure brings a lot of color to my life. When you meet someone who brings you into their family and shows love, understanding, and compassion, don't take them for granted. Those are the kind of people you are going to need in your life because they will bring you up when you are down. They will give you a leg up when times get tough. You can't go through life on your own, but when you have family and God, you can go through anything.

My relationship with the good Lord wasn't always great. I grew up throwing rocks at the heavens because of my childhood. I had nothing but anger and hatred toward God. But when Leah and her parents came into my life, they led me in the right direction and showed me that God really is about love.

One Bible verse that stuck with me all these years was from the book of John 1:11-12. "He came to his own and his own people did not receive him. But to all who did receive him, who believed, in his name, he gave the right to become children of God." That just goes to show that no matter what kind of background we come from, God loves us unconditionally, even after all those years when I thought He didn't love me at all.

I thank God for the way my life is now. I'm healthy. I've got a great head on my shoulders, and I'm still alive! Injured but alive. He brought people into my life who have given me more than I could ask for. I praise God for that indeed.

As for Leah, Karen, and Frank, I will always show them love, understanding, and compassion the same way they have with me because that's what family does for each other.

That's also what God does for us.

As all God's people say, "God is good all the time. All the time, God is good!"